MAIL ORDER BRIDE

Montana Miracle

Echo Canyon Brides
Book 10

LINDA BRIDEY

Dedication

This book is dedicated to all of my faithful readers, without whom I would be nothing. I thank you for the support, reviews, love, and friendship you have shown me as we have gone through this journey together. I am truly blessed to have such a wonderful readership.

Contents

Chapter One 1

Chapter Two.................................... 14

Chapter Three 23

Chapter Four 31

Chapter Five 38

Chapter Six 47

Chapter Seven 55

Chapter Eight 63

Chapter Nine................................ 70

Chapter Ten.................................... 76

Chapter Eleven................................. 85

Chapter Twelve.................... 92

Chapter Thirteen 99

Chapter Fourteen 107

Chapter Fifteen 112

Chapter Sixteen......................... 119

Chapter Seventeen 127

Chapter Eighteen..................... 136

Chapter Nineteen 143

Chapter Twenty.................... 150

Chapter Twenty-One.............. 159

Epilogue 166

Linda's Other Books.................. 175

Cast of Characters 177

Connect With Linda 179

About Linda Bridey.................. 180

Chapter One

"I've never had this happen. I don't know what to do," Sofia Carter said. She sat having supper with her sister, Leah, and her brother-in-law, Lucky Quinn.

Leah, who was deaf, signed, "I think it's wonderful and you should be flattered."

"I *am* flattered," Sofia said. "It's just rather unexpected, that's all."

She watched her three-year-old niece, Lily, as Leah helped her eat. The toddler had Leah's dark hair and Lucky's gray eyes. Sofia adored her and her nephew, Otto, who had recently turned nine.

"Which one do you like the best?" Leah asked.

Sofia tucked a strand of golden-blonde hair behind her ear. "I like them both for different reasons. Travis is handsome, down-to-earth, a good father and very kind. Captain Rawlins is also handsome, gentlemanly, charismatic, and has a good job. Not that Travis doesn't, of course. I don't know which invitation to accept!"

Lucky chuckled. "It's terrible to be wanted by more than one man. Otto has the same problem, only with girls, don't ya, lad?"

Otto grinned, his dark eyes gleaming. "Aye." He liked mimicking his father's Irish accent.

Leah asked, "How many admirers do you have right now?"

Otto ticked them off silently on his fingers. "Five."

They laughed with him.

"Five?" Sofia asked. "Who are they?"

"Dewdrop, Clara, Dorie, Bella, and Gray Dove," Otto replied.

Lucky laughed. "He can't help it. He gets it from me and he doesn't even hafta try. Neither did I."

Leah said, "Shame on you for playing on women's affections."

The handsome Irishman put an arm around Leah and kissed her cheek. "Don't be jealous. Ya know yer the only lass I love."

Leah blushed as she giggled and pushed him away playfully.

Sofia asked Otto, "How do you decide who to pay attention to?"

"I don't. I let *them* pay attention to *me*," he said. "That's what you should do. Let Travis and Captain Rawlins fight for you. Whoever treats you the best wins."

Leah gaped at him for a moment. "Is that what you do? Lucky, did you teach him that?"

"I didn't," Lucky said. "But I have a hunch who did. Otto, don't be takin' advice on girls from Marvin. Plus, ya better not let Fiona hear ya say such things."

Otto shook his head. "I won't. Fi's the best of them all, anyways. Uncle Marvin didn't tell me that. Wild Wind says that how the girls in tribes do it. The brave that gives the most gifts and treats her the best wins her heart. I can't help it if girls like me," he said, shrugging.

Sofia smiled. "He might be only nine, but he might be right. I could go out with each of them once and then make up my mind. I know Travis, but I don't really know Zeb."

Leah said, "That sound reasonable."

Sofia said, "Zeb asked me first, so I'll go to dinner with him first."

"That's fair," Lucky said. "But here's somethin' ya should consider; the captain is in his early forties and might not be thinkin' about havin' little ones at this point in his life. Ya should find that out right away because I know ya want some. Travis wants more. He loves Pauline to death, but he's always wanted more kids."

Sofia said, "Oh. You're right. I hadn't thought about that. Thank you, Lucky."

"Yer welcome."

"We have new boarders again," Sofia said. She now worked full-time at the Hanover House as their housekeeper and cook. She loved the Hanovers and enjoyed living in the private suite of rooms they'd given her. Since she had off on Sundays, she usually ate supper with her family.

Their whole evening was spent having fun and visiting and Sofia enjoyed every moment of it. During the week, she didn't have a lot of time to see them because of her work schedule. Leah owned a cobbler shop in town and Lucky had his sheep farm to tend, which was a more than full-time job. Otto was big enough to help with a few chores after school and on the weekends, but the majority of the work was done by Lucky. During the summer, their friend and Echo's schoolteacher, Adam Harris, worked there, too, which was a huge help to Lucky.

Win and Erin also lived on the farm, but Win's vet practice was taking off now, not to mention his barbershop. Therefore, his time on the farm was limited. Lucky was looking for help, but hadn't found anyone he liked yet. His friend, Arliss, also helped, but he'd been out of town a lot lately, doing undercover work of some sort or another for the government. He never said and Lucky never asked, knowing that Arliss couldn't have told him even if he'd wanted to.

Around eight o'clock, Sofia took her leave, refusing Lucky's offer to see her home. He always wanted to ride with her, but she was capable of getting home on her own. Since moving to Echo a couple of years ago, she'd become very self-sufficient and she was proud of herself.

She trotted her horse along on the frigid, late October night, enjoying the ride since she was bundled up well. The cold snap hadn't broken yet and it felt more like December than the end of October.

Someone streaked across the road a short ways up ahead and she stopped her horse, waiting to see if they reappeared, but whoever it was must have continued through the dense woods. She rode on, but in a little while, she heard a horse approaching from the rear and she moved over on the road a little. After the recent discovery that a madman was on the loose around Echo, who had murdered at least six women, she was a little nervous about who might be coming, but she was carrying her pistol that Lucky had taught her how to use.

"Excuse me, ma'am," a man said.

"Hello, Captain Rawlins," she said recognizing his uniform.

"Miss Carter, how nice to see you again," he said, smiling.

"Likewise. How may I help you?"

"Have you seen either Skyhawk or Dog Star by chance?" he asked. He was plainly putout.

"Uh oh. Did they sneak out again?"

"Yes. I have better things to do than play babysitter to a couple of wayward boys."

Sofia hid her smile. "Well, someone crossed the road in front of me a little while back, but I couldn't see who it was."

"It was most likely one of them and where one is, the other isn't far behind. Of course, their other two cohorts were most likely with them, too," Zeb said. "I'm not going to go traipsing around in the woods after them. You would think they'd learned their lesson about that after discovering a dead body, but it seems as though they haven't. I know two boys who are going to lose some privileges."

"Do you like children, Zeb?" Sofia blurted and wished she could take back the words. She hadn't meant to ask him right then, but the subject had already been on her mind.

One of his dark brows rose. "Yes, I do."

"Just not Indian children."

He heard the note of censure in her voice. "I like *all* children, regardless of race. I just prefer that they behave and those two try my patience every day. You've no idea what I go through with them and I have a hunch that Porter is in on their pranks, simply because his father doesn't like me."

Zeb was often at odds with Sheriff Evan Taft and his deputies, Shadow Earnest, and, Thad McIntyre, Porter's father.

4

"I don't think that they don't like you personally, they just don't like the military. Maybe you could show them that you don't represent the army as a whole. Try to show them that although you wear the uniform, you don't view Indians in the same way that other military officers do," Sofia suggested.

Zeb was a military man through-and-through and he had trouble separating himself as a man from the uniform. This was the reason he'd never married, and since turning forty-three, he'd begun contemplating what his life would be like after he retired. He saw a cold, lonely future ahead, something he didn't relish.

Upon moving to Echo to guard the newly built Indian school, an unwanted post, the slower pace hadn't sat well with him. He was used to more action, more men to command, and work to be done. Therefore, if he wasn't on night duty, there wasn't much to do. He went to Spike's now and again, but it was unpleasant if Evan was around. The sheriff's intense dislike of him was almost palpable, and Zeb wasn't enamored of him, either. Therefore, he generally stayed away.

With more time on his hands, he'd thought about finding a wife; a woman to love and share his life with. The only problem was that single women were still scarce around Echo, which was why men had begun to advertise for brides a few years ago.

He'd run into Sofia quite often in town and had taken a fancy to the young woman. She was beautiful, intelligent, and a hard worker. He knew that there was more to her than that and wanted to get to know her better. So, he'd finally called on her.

"I see what you're saying, but honestly, I'm not sure how to go about that. I've served for so long that there are times when I'm not sure where the uniform ends and I begin. If I can't figure it out, how can they?"

Sofia chuckled. "Start by spending more time out of the uniform then."

Zeb grinned. "If I do that, Sheriff Taft will arrest me for indecency."

His witty remark caught her off guard and she laughed. "Yes, he would, but it would give everyone something to talk about. Are you on duty tonight?"

"No."

"Then why are you still wearing your uniform?"

Zeb said, "I only have my jacket and pants on. I had everything but my pants off …" He trailed off into laughter. "That's more information than you need."

Sofia said, "Well, yes, a little bit, but I understand now. I'm just saying that you need to show them that you're more than just a soldier."

Am I? Zeb suddenly realized that he didn't know who he was outside of being a soldier. He'd been one since he'd turned eighteen. "I suppose you're right."

Sofia saw that they were drawing close to town. Fidgeting with her reins, she said, "Regarding your invitation to dinner, Wednesday would be fine if that suits you."

Her acceptance thrilled him. "Wednesday suits just fine. Is seven acceptable?"

"Yes," Sofia said.

"Wonderful," he said as they arrived at the back of the boarding house.

Sofia was surprised when he dismounted with her.

"Allow me to put your horse away for you," he said, holding her horse even though it was unnecessary.

She was touched by his gallant gesture. Her ex-fiancé, Gary, hadn't done things like that for her. "All right. Thank you."

"My pleasure. You go in out of the cold now. Have a good night," he said.

Looking at him in the moonlight, she thought that he was a remarkably good-looking man with his black hair and dark eyes. He was strong and fit with slightly chiseled features. "Goodnight, Captain."

"Zeb," he said.

"Very well. Goodnight, Zeb," she said, smiling.

"Goodnight, Sofia."

As she walked up the walkway leading to her door, he thought it was a good sign that she hadn't minded him calling her by her given name. Whistling a little, he took her horse into the stable and put it away.

When he arrived home later, Zeb walked up the narrow, brick walk to the outside door of his rooms at the school. He'd just gotten his keys out of his coat pocket when his feet went right out from under him. Backwards he went, his head smacking against the ice-glazed walkway. Pain exploded inside his brain and he lost consciousness.

From behind a nearby tree, Dog Star and Skyhawk grinned and stifled their laughter. When the captain didn't get up, they sobered.

"He is not moving," Dog Star said, in Cheyenne.

"It is a trick," Skyhawk said. "He is playing dead so he can catch us."

Dog Star said, "I do not think so. We must help him."

The boys ran to the fallen man.

"Captain?" Dog Star said in English. There was enough moonlight for him to see that Zeb's eyes were closed. He leaned down and heard the man's breathing. "Captain Rawlins?" He shook him a little, but Zeb didn't rouse.

Skyhawk said, "I'll go get Cade and then go for Dr. Erin. You stay with him."

"Ok." Tears formed in Dog Star's eyes. "I'm sorry, Captain. Please don't die. We didn't mean for you to get hurt. I'm sorry."

"All right, all right!" Corporal Cade Hadley shouted when someone banged loudly on his door a second time. "Hold your horses!" He hopped over to the door as he pulled on a pair of jeans and opened it still shirtless. "Skyhawk. Why are you—?"

"You gotta come quick! Captain Rawlins is hurt," Skyhawk said, panic in his dark eyes. "He's outside his door on the ground. Dog Star is with him. I'm going to get Dr. Erin." He ran for the barn before Cade could respond.

Cade threw on his coat and ran around to the other side of the large log structure, finding Dog Star kneeling on the frozen ground next to Zeb.

"What the hell happened?" he demanded. "Never mind. Go light a lamp and get a fire goin'. We have to get him warm."

Dog Star raced to Zeb's door, but it wouldn't open. "It's locked. I don't know where the keys are."

Cade ran over to the door and made the boy stand back. He kicked the door open, wood splintering as the lock tore through the doorjamb. "Now get that lamp lit and a fire built!"

Dog Star hurried to comply while Cade got his arms under Zeb and lifted him up carefully. He didn't like moving him before he could be examined, but the man couldn't be left outside in the freezing cold until Erin could get there. Zeb wasn't a small man, so carrying him inside was no easy feat. Cade prevented Zeb's head from hitting anything as he took him into the bedroom and laid him on the bed once Dog Star turned it down.

Cade started looking Zeb over. Putting his hand under Zeb's head, he felt a warm wetness and his hand came away bloody. Dog Star blanched at the sight of it.

"Get me some towels!" Cade ordered. The boy didn't move. "Dog Star! Towels! Move!"

Dog Star rushed into the small washroom, grabbed a couple of towels, and brought them back. Cade took them and began applying pressure to the wound. "What happened, and don't you dare lie to me, or you'll get the worst beatin' you've ever had."

Knowing that Cade didn't hit kids, the fact that he'd even said he would told Dog Star how angry he was.

"It was just a joke. W-we didn't mean to hurt him. We poured a little water over the walk," Dog Star said, more tears falling from his eyes. "Will he be ok?"

Fury sparkled in Cade's blue eyes. "I don't know. I hope so."

"I'm sorry."

"Go get Miss Benscotter and Mr. Burkhart."

Dog Star ran through the small parlor in the suite, opened the interior door, and left the captain's rooms.

Cade leaned down close to Zeb. "Zeb, it's Cade. Come on and wake up," he said, lightly patting Zeb's face. "Don't die on me, Zeb. Dear Lord, please don't let him die."

Zeb woke up slowly and wished he hadn't. His head throbbed and nausea gripped him. He tried to swallow, but his mouth was so dry that it was almost impossible. Barely opening his eyes, he tried to get his bearings. Cautiously turning his head, he recognized his bedroom.

"Captain, try not to move around much," Erin said, coming into his line of sight. "Can you see me?"

"Yes," he whispered. "What happened?"

"You fell on some ice and hit your head very hard. Is your vision blurry or do you have double vision?"

"A little blurry, but there's only one of you."

Erin smiled. "Good. Are you nauseous?"

"Yes and my head is killing me."

"I'm not surprised. As hard as you hit, you're lucky to be alive. I had to shave a patch of your scalp so I could stitch up the laceration to it. Your hair will grow back, though," she said. "Are you thirsty?"

"Yes."

Erin helped him take a couple of sips of water. "Just rest, Zeb. It's the best thing for you. I'll have someone make you some ginger tea to help settle your stomach."

"Ok."

In moments, he slipped back into slumber.

Lance Burkhart, the school administrator, glared at Dog Star and Skyhawk, an expression they didn't often see on his face.

"You've put the school in jeopardy with this stupid antic of yours. We could be shut down because you didn't appreciate the chance you've been given here. You're lucky that Captain Rawlins didn't die, or you'd be going to jail for murder. You might still see jail time if he decides to press charges.

And if by some miracle he doesn't, you still might be kicked out. I haven't made up my mind about that," he said.

Skyhawk said, "We had a chance on the reservation, too. It wasn't our choice to be separated from our families and be forced to go to one of these schools."

"That's not the issue right now. Would your parents approve of what you've done? You unnecessarily put a man's life in jeopardy. It's not like putting salt instead of sugar in someone's coffee or some other harmless prank. You made his walkway icy, for God's sake! He could have broken a leg or an arm or anything!"

Dog Star said, "I'm sorry. It was my idea. I only poured a little bit on it. Just a small spot; I thought he'd just trip a little." He felt utterly horrible about what he'd done. "I deserve to go to jail."

Lance was glad to see some remorse from the boy, but Skyhawk was defiant to the core. His dark gaze clashed with Lance's. "Skyhawk, this chip you have on your shoulder has gotten you in scalding hot water. Everything depends on Captain Rawlins. You'll stay in your rooms except for meals, school or doing chores. You'll do whatever you're told to in order to help the captain get well again."

"And if we don't?" Skyhawk said.

Lance said, "I'll send you back to Ft. Shaw."

Fear flashed in Skyhawk's eyes. Echo's Indian school was a much better place to be than Ft. Shaw's. There they'd been forced to cut their hair, wear white man's clothing, and to accept a different religion. They'd also sometimes been beaten or starved for bad behavior.

In Echo, they had many freedoms; wearing their native clothing, speaking their native tongue, and no one had raised a hand to them. The food was great, they liked their teacher, and the other employees all treated them with kindness and affection. If they went back to Ft. Shaw, their life there would be even more miserable than before.

Lance saw his advantage and pressed it. "I'll take you there myself if you don't do what I'm telling you to do."

Someone knocked on his office door.

"Come in," he called.

The president of the Indian schoolboard, Wild Wind, entered. He said, "I need to borrow them."

"Be my guest," Lance said.

Wild Wind's black eyes glittered with barely restrained anger as he clamped a hand on the back of each boy's neck. "Move," he ordered.

He forced them ahead of him until they arrived outside Zeb's suite. "Be quiet in here." They went in and Wild Wind pushed them into Zeb's bedroom. "Do you see what you've done to this man who has only helped keep you safe since he's been here?"

The boys were horrified by Zeb's appearance. His head had been bandaged and it looked like he had two black eyes. There was also a bruise on his right temple. Skyhawk tried to look away, but Wild Wind wouldn't let him. He grabbed Skyhawk's hair and forced him to gaze at the captain.

"This is because you can't let go of your bitterness. I don't like the military much, either, but this was stupid and cruel. I am ashamed of you!" Wild Wind whispered furiously.

Skyhawk greatly respected Wild Wind and Arrow, his fellow Cheyenne, and Wild Wind's disapproval cut him worse than any criticism from someone else.

"I'm sorry," Skyhawk said in English

"You'll do whatever Lance tells you to do. This just shows the people who hate us that they're right about us. They could say that you were trying to kill Zeb," Wild Wind said.

As Wild Wind quietly berated the boys, Zeb woke up. He'd heard enough to understand that they had caused his accident and while he knew he should be angry, he didn't have the strength at the moment. Even in his slightly clouded state Zeb knew what power he wielded. He'd been in the military and around law enforcement too long not to.

Although he knew the two youths weren't his greatest admirers, he doubted that they'd meant to be malicious. Therefore, he decided not to risk the school or their futures by turning them in. Despite his stern exterior, he did have a heart. However, that didn't mean he was going to let them completely off the hook.

"Gentleman," he whispered, surprised by how much the quiet action hurt his head. "Come here so I don't have to yell."

Wild Wind nudged the boys forward until they stood close to Zeb's bed. Dog Star wore a terrified expression and fear glimmered in Skyhawk's eyes even though his face remained stony.

"So you decided to play another trick on me, hmm?"

Dog Star said, "It was my idea. I didn't mean for you to get hurt. I'm sorry, Captain."

Zeb stared into Skyhawk's eyes until the boy's dropped. "I'm sorry, too. You were just supposed to trip a little, not go down like a ton of bricks."

Maybe it was his concussion, but Zeb found it funny that Skyhawk would somehow turn the fault for the incident around like that. He let out a soft laugh and regretted it. "Well, I'm sorry I messed up your plans. I'll do better the next time you try to kill me." He grabbed his head as more laughter escaped him.

The boys looked at each other in confusion and then at Wild Wind, surprised to see that he was smiling.

When Zeb's mirth subsided, he said, "I'm not going to contact the military over your stupidity, but once I'm better, I'm going to teach you a lesson about doing this sort of thing. Wild Wind, don't tell anyone in town what actually happened. I don't want any of the children or the school to come to any trouble. Don't tell anyone where the ice came from. It's perfectly plausible for there to be a little here and there."

Skyhawk's brow puckered. "Why would you protect us like that?"

Zeb smiled wanly as Sofia's words came back to him. He was surprised he'd remembered their conversation given his injury. "Because although you're stubborn, argumentative, conceited, and foolhardy, I happen to like you. I'm not sure why, but I do. As Wild Wind said, do whatever Mr. Burkhart says, but when I'm better, your asses belong to me and you'll be sorrier than you could ever imagine. Now go so I can rest. Wild Wind, will you please stay?"

"You go to class," Wild Wind said, "And you'd better do everything Mrs. Emerson says—or else."

The boys nodded and left the room.

"Do the other students know that they were involved?" Zeb asked.

"Not yet. They don't know why Dog Star and Skyhawk were called in. All they know is that they snuck out last night and then found you," Wild Wind said.

"Good. I'm glad you protected them that way. As much as I didn't want this post, I can see the good you're doing here and it would be a shame for the school to close. If any of the Indian-haters got wind of this, they'd report it right away. Please ask the staff to stay quiet, too," Zeb said.

"We've already done that. Thank you for being considerate of the school and those boys," Wild Wind said. "I'll enjoy seeing how you punish them."

"You approve of that?" Zeb asked.

Wild Wind nodded. "They need to make restitution to you. In our culture, the wronged party decides what that restitution will be. So I think it's only right that you punish them as you see fit."

Zeb smiled. "Then be prepared to be amused."

Wild Wind smiled. "Get some rest and thanks again."

Zeb held up a hand briefly as Wild Wind left. With a sigh, he closed his eyes and prayed for his head to stop hurting.

Chapter Two

Josie Taft looked across their parlor at her husband. Instead of working on the new sweater he'd been knitting for Win and Erin's burro, Sugar, the project rested on his lap. Although his green eyes appeared to be staring intently at the window, she knew that his mind was working on something law enforcement related.

Most likely, it was the case of all the murdered women that had been found at the end of the summer. It was what he thought about most of the time, his drive to catch the monster responsible consuming him. Evan's perseverance when on the track of a criminal was one of the things that singled him out as one of the best lawmen in the Midwest. He never let a crime go, even if he didn't solve it right away.

It was one of the reasons he kept careful records and demanded that his deputies do the same thing. In the past, he'd proven the usefulness of writing reports. Sometimes things clicked in his brain when a new piece of information came to light that turned out to be related to a prior crime. Often when he went back to a report, he found a piece of the puzzle that snapped everything into place, enabling him to lock up some piece of scum.

"Ma!" their six-year-old daughter, Julie said, coming down the stairs. "Ma!"

Josie said, "Shh. Not so loud. Wyatt's asleep."

Julie trotted over to her chair. "He sleeps too much," she complained of her two-year-old brother.

Josie smiled. "He's little yet. That's why he goes to bed so early. You'll be going to bed soon, too."

"Yep. That's why I put my nightie on," she said. "When's Uncle Shadow comin' to see me?"

Josie glanced at Evan whose attention was now on Julia. "Well, he's been busy, honey. I'm sure he'll come see you soon."

Evan frowned, thinking about his friend. Their relationship was strained at the moment, but only because Shadow refused to talk to him about whatever Thad and Marvin wouldn't tell him. He and Marvin were never going to be close friends, but Thad's continued silence on the matter greatly disturbed him. Their friendship also wasn't as close as it normally would was.

All of the tension in the sheriff's office every day was impeding Evan's ability to think clearly, which was why he used whatever quiet time he had at home to concentrate on the toughest case he'd faced in a while.

Julia's big blue eyes filled with sadness. "Don't he love me anymore?"

Evan looked at the ceiling and decided that he was going to give Shadow a piece of his mind in the morning. Just because some of the adults weren't getting along didn't mean that the kids should suffer. They didn't understand what was going on. All they knew was that some of their favorite people weren't around at the moment. He also decided to press the issue hard with Shadow. It was time to end this.

Julia climbed up on his lap and he hugged her close before telling her a funny story from his boyhood. She yawned before he finished, so he took her up to bed to tell her the rest of it. It wasn't long before she fell asleep. Evan sat on the edge of her bed, watching her pretty little face as she slept. His love for his children ran deep and as he thought about the monster who lurked somewhere in Echo, he vowed to catch them and make the town a safer place for all.

When Shadow walked into the sheriff's office the next day, he saw a determined expression on Evan's face.

"You look rather pensive," he remarked to his boss.

"I am. Julia misses you. So do Rebel and Wyatt."

Shadow sighed as he poured a cup of coffee from the pot on the small stove. "I'll bring the family and come over tomorrow night."

"Before you do that, I'm going to appeal to you as your friend. Forget that I'm a sheriff. Talk to me the way you would any other friend and tell me what the hell is going on. I'm sick and tired of all this tension because you won't tell me, Thad won't tell me, and Marvin won't tell me. I understand that Thad is being loyal to you. Give *me* the chance to be loyal to you. I might surprise you, Shadow. Please?"

Shadow walked over to the window and put the blind down so he could take off his dark glasses. He sat down at his desk and met Evan's gaze. He, too, was tired of the strain between them. Evan's friendship was important to him, but could Evan separate himself from his badge and understand? Was he willing to risk that? He knew they had that immunity deal between them, but would Evan honor it once he knew his secret?

"Do you promise to listen to me only as a friend and not as a sheriff? Can you really shut down that part of yourself?"

Evan spread his hands wide. "That's what I've been telling you! Yes, I promise."

Shadow gathered his thoughts. "You already know what our parents did to me."

"Yeah."

"What you don't know is that we killed them," Shadow said. He waited for Evan's reaction.

Evan laughed and ran a hand over his face. "Is that what this has been about? I already figured that out, Shadow. I don't know how you killed them, but I just knew that they didn't die overseas. It made much more sense that you guys would've taken justice into your own hands, and I gotta tell you that I don't blame you after the sheer hell they put you through."

Shadow stared at him in surprise. "You knew?"

Evan leaned back and crossed his arms over his chest. "I think sometimes you forget who you're dealing with. I'm not a famous sheriff for nothing."

Shadow smiled because it was true. Evan's closed case record was exemplary and his reputation had grown since he'd taken over as Echo's sheriff at the age of twenty-two.

"Would you like to know how we killed them?"

"Hell, yeah. I hope you made them suffer the way they made you suffer," Evan said.

Shadow also sometimes forgot that Evan could be bloodthirsty. "We drugged them and hauled them down to my cage. We tortured them for days. I'll spare you the exact details, but suffice it to say that it wasn't pretty. Then we left them down there for several months to die and rot. After that it was easy to pound them into dust with sledgehammers and scatter their remains in the swamp. That's the whole story."

Shadow was further surprised when a grin spread across Evan's face. "Boy, you guys really are deadly and twisted. That's great thinking. That's another reason I hired you."

Shadow arched an eyebrow. "So you're not going to arrest me?"

"Hell, no. It was a long time ago and we have that agreement. But first and foremost, you're my friend. I can't believe we are sometimes. But even though you're twisted, you're likeable and more human than you think you are. You're not an animal, Shadow. You're a guy who was dealt a horrible hand, but look at the way your life has turned out. You gotta let all of that go once and for all."

Shadow hated it, but Evan's support brought tears to his eyes. "I owe you an apology. I should have trusted you enough to tell you all of this. I'm sorry. I'm just not used to people believing in me. Bree and my brother do, but I'm leery about trusting other people."

Evan nodded. "I can understand why you might feel that way, but you can tell me anything. That's what being friends means. If I didn't believe in you, I wouldn't have hired you."

Shadow chuckled. "So my diabolical mind is an attribute on the job?"

"Yeah. You can think like the sick scum out there, no offense. It's a valuable insight and you've proven that on several occasions. Hiring you is one of the best things I ever did. You can trust Thad, too." Evan made a face. "As much as I hate to stick up for him, Marvin's been through a lot, too. He needed someone to talk to and I guess Thad was his choice, for whatever reason. You did, too. Don't you feel better?"

"I must admit that I do."

"Good. Get rid of that cage. I'll help you," Evan said. "It has nothing to do with your life anymore. You have a beautiful, loving, wife, adorable kids and you're trying for more. You have a job that you love, friends and you're making more all the time. You gotta put this to rest. Don't let your parents keep having power over you. You got your revenge. Let that be enough."

Shadow looked up at the ceiling as he blinked back tears again. He considered Evan's remarks and saw the wisdom in them. "You're right. They've wielded power over me long enough. You'll really help us dismantle the cage? Where would we take it?"

"Bernie's Junkyard. He'll melt it down and use it to make something else. Now, something else; talk to Marvin. Work things out with him. He's your brother and he loves you. He was traumatized, too. I think you forget that sometimes," Evan said.

"You surprise me, Evan." Shadow smiled. "I'll deal with Marvin, but you should, too. What happened with Louise is over and done, the same way that what happened to me is over and done. If I have to let it go, so do you. After all, he did you a favor. You were meant to be with Josie and you have beautiful kids, too. You would've never been happy with Louise and you know it."

Evan scowled and looked away. Everything Shadow had just said was true. He hated to say it, but Marvin had proven himself trustworthy on several occasions, but Evan wondered if he'd ever completely trust Marvin again.

Giving Shadow a displeased look, he grudgingly said, "Ok. I'll try."

Shadow cocked his head a little and Evan rolled his eyes. "Ok, I'll try hard. That's the best I can do right now."

"I'll take it," Shadow said.

The door opened and Thad came in. He shivered. "Brrr! It's cold out there. Don't try to take a leak out there. Things are liable to freeze."

"Nice of you to show up, old timer," Evan said.

Thad narrowed his eyes. "Old timer, my ass. I can still run circles around you any day of the week."

"Yeah, yeah. Get some coffee and sit down. We've been having a nice conversation about the Unholy Bookends pounding their parents into dust and throwing them in the swamp," Evan said.

Thad just stared at Shadow. "Is that what you did with them? Marvin said you killed them, but he didn't tell me how. God, I'm glad all of this is getting out in the open. I can't stand all this secret crap."

Shadow sighed and repeated his story to Thad. The other deputy got his coffee and sat down. "Good for you boys! They got what they deserved as far as I'm concerned. Now you need to get rid of that cage and seal up that room. Nail that door shut and cover it with concrete. Over and done for good."

"You've seen it?" Evan asked.

Thad nodded. "Yeah, and I wish I hadn't. Marvin showed me." He pointed at Shadow. "Shut your yapper about it. He had a good reason and it did him good. It made me see that he's more human than I gave him credit for. We ain't buddies, but I don't wanna beat the crap out of him as much as I did before."

Shadow held up his hands in surrender. "If it makes you feel better, Evan, Win hasn't seen it, either."

Evan's jaw clenched. "But he knew about it all?"

"Yes. Marvin told him."

Shadow suddenly found himself the victim of a siege of missiles in the form of pencils as Evan whipped a bunch of them at him. Shadow ducked as the pencils bounced off his forearms and chest. When he was out of pencils, Evan threw the empty tin cup they'd been in at Shadow. It bounced off Shadow's forehead and clattered to the floor.

Jerry Belker, Echo's mayor, opened the door and saw all of the pencils on the floor and took in the three laughing men. "Is this how you solve crimes?"

Thad said, "Yep. It helps us think better."

"Mmm hmm. Good. So what have your brilliant minds come up with about this killer?" Jerry asked. "I got people askin' me left and right about the investigation."

Evan frowned and rubbed his forehead. "The problem is that the satanic symbol on their thighs is the only clue so far. Erin performed autopsies on them all and there was nothing out of the ordinary about them. The most recent murder was about four months ago by Erin's estimation.

"We've been working on finding anyone who's into the occult. We have some other people on the alert, too. I've been in touch with several other sheriffs and none of them have had this sort of murder in their jurisdiction. They'll let me know if they do, but I hope they don't. So tell these people the same thing I do; we're working hard on it and we won't rest until we catch them."

"Ok. I appreciate the update," Jerry said. "You won't have to worry about Captain Rawlins botherin' you for a while."

"How come?" Evan asked.

"Well, seems he slipped on some ice last night and hit his head real hard when he fell. He has one heck of a concussion," Jerry replied. "Erin said if he'd have hit it any harder, he'd be dead."

Evan could hardly stand Zeb, but he still felt badly that the captain had been hurt. "Is he gonna be all right?"

"Erin thinks with some rest, he'll recover just fine," Jerry said.

"I'm glad to hear it," Evan said.

Thad grunted. "Maybe it'll knock some niceness into him."

"I doubt it," Shadow remarked as he picked up the pencils Evan had thrown at him.

Jerry gave them all a disapproving look. "Try to get along with him. It'll make my life easier if you do."

Evan said, "I get along with him just fine when he stays out of my business. I know my job and I don't need his interference. He's not trained in investigating. I don't tell him how to fight a battle, do I?"

"In case you didn't notice, he doesn't have a regiment to take into battle. He's probably bored," Jerry said.

"No, he thinks he's high and mighty since he's military," Thad protested. "Evan's right. He doesn't do investigating and has no business trying to butt in. We don't answer to him and the sooner he learns that the better."

Jerry shook his head. "Well, instead of trying to prove who has the biggest cojones, maybe you should think about working together. I don't care who solves this thing; I just want it solved. Can you do that for the town?"

"You mean you want me to ask him for help?" Evan said, bristling.

"Yes. Whatever it takes to catch this monster. If you haven't solved it by the time he's better, see if he and Cade will help out," Jerry said.

Shadow growled. "Haven't you been listening? They don't investigate crime. They order people about and fight wars."

"Well, they do know strategy," Thad said.

"Whose side are you on?" Evan and Shadow said in unison.

Jerry laughed. "You two are getting too close. Like I said, gentlemen. Whatever it takes."

"Who made you boss?" Evan groused.

"You did when you voted for me," Jerry said, stepping through the doorway.

"We can correct that!" Evan shouted after him.

Jerry just waved and went on his way. Evan scowled, his arms resting across his chest. He looked at Thad when the deputy laughed.

"You used to look just like that when you were a kid and your pa told you to go to bed," Thad said. "I guess some things never change."

Evan fired his last pencil at Thad, who deflected it at the last second before it hit him in the eye. "Hey! Are you tryin' to blind me?"

"No. I was aiming for your mouth to shut you up," Evan said, standing up. "I'll make nice and go see Zeb. I'm the sheriff so I have to put aside my differences—oh, hell. You know what I'm sayin'. Someone go out on patrol while I'm gone. I don't care who it is. You're big boys—sort of."

Thad and Shadow watched him go and then Shadow threw a pencil, hitting Thad in the ear.

"Just for that you get to go out on patrol," Thad said, lighting up a cigarette.

Shadow stood and stretched before beginning to dance. Thad watched him as though he'd lost his mind.

"What sort of dance is that?" he asked.

"Salsa," Shadow said, moving his hips suggestively. "Bree loves it when I do this for her. You should let me show you how to do it."

Thad raised an eyebrow. "That's all right. I don't think my hips will work like that at my age."

Shadow stopped dancing and put on his coat. "Very well. Just think of how entertaining it would be for Jessie. I bid you adieu."

Thad puffed thoughtfully on his cigarette and then looked contemplatively at his pelvis. Then he shook his head. "Nope. I'm liable to throw out a hip."

Chapter Three

Evan looked at Zeb, who slept soundly, and frowned. He might have his differences with the man, but he took no pleasure from Zeb being injured. He was about to leave when Sofia came into the room. She looked at him and then Zeb and let out a small gasp.

"He looks awful," she whispered, coming closer, carrying a basket.

Evan nodded. "He took one heck of a knock on the noggin. Jerry said it was bad, but seeing it's different than hearing it."

"Yes. Arthur told me about him. It's strange that he slipped on ice. We haven't had any rain or snow lately," she remarked.

One of Evan's eyebrows rose. She was right. *So where did the ice come from?* "Maybe some of the dew froze on the walkway." He didn't really believe that, though.

Sofia shrugged. "Well, I'm relieved that he'll recover. I brought him some cinnamon muffins."

Evan leaned over, trying to look in the basket. Sofia saw him and smiled. "Would you like one?"

"I don't want to take his muffins," Evan said. "They do smell good, though."

Sofia picked one out of the basket and handed it to him. "I think one for the sheriff is all right."

Evan smiled. "Thanks. I'll come back to see him this evening. Take care, Sofia. And don't be traveling around alone at night like you did last night. It's not safe."

Sofia said, "I have a gun and besides, I met up with Zeb and he accompanied me home. So I was perfectly safe."

"I'm glad to hear it. I'll see ya," Evan said.

Sofia sat in a chair a short distance away from Zeb's bed. It wasn't proper to be alone in his bedroom with him, but the door was open and she couldn't help that there wasn't anyone with him right at that moment. Besides, he wasn't in any shape to do anything inappropriate.

His bandaged head and darkened eyes looked dreadful and Sofia felt badly for him. It was strange to see him in a sleeping shirt when she'd only ever seen him in his uniform. He looked vulnerable and it brought a feeling of tenderness out in her.

Zeb stirred, opening his eyes. He saw Sofia and offered her a weak smile. "Hello, Sofia."

She moved closer to him. "Hello, Zeb. How are you feeling?"

"I've been better, but seeing you helps."

She smiled. "Even with a big bump on your head you're flattering me. Is there anything I can get you?"

"Perhaps some water."

Looking around, Sofia saw a picture and cup on his dresser. She poured a cup and carefully helped him drink.

"Thank you. It was kind of you to come visit me," he said.

"I'm sorry about what happened. I didn't know there was any ice last night," Sofia said.

"I certainly wasn't expecting any," he said wryly. "Don't worry. I'll be better before long, although, I think we'll have to postpone our outing."

Sofia said, "Yes, but it's just a temporary setback."

After a few more minutes, Sofia decided that she should leave and let him get his rest. She promised to come back the next day and left the basket of muffins with him. Zeb looked after her as she left, his irritation piqued because they weren't going to go out to dinner when they'd planned. He appeased his anger by thinking up more punishment for the boys who'd put him in this condition.

⌒﹏⌒

Travis Desmond strolled up the back walkway to the kitchen at the Hanover House, carrying a box. He hummed a little as he mounted the steps onto the small porch and knocked on the door.

He smiled at Sofia when she opened it. "Howdy, Miss Sofia," he said. "You're lookin' pretty today."

Sofia blushed a little. "Thank you, Travis. Come in."

He entered the kitchen and inhaled a delicious aroma. "Mmm. What's cooking?"

"A ham," she said, eyeing the box he carried. "What do you have there?"

"Oh." He sat it down on the table and opened it. "I remembered you telling me that you wanted to get some fresh herbs. I had to run out to the Terranovas' place for Marvin and I got a few small plants for you."

She watched him take out little pots of oregano, thyme, rosemary, and basil. Then he pulled out a little potted fern and handed it to her.

"I thought you might enjoy that since you're so handy with plants."

"Thank you for everything. How—"

"No, no. You don't owe me a thing," he said. "I know you'll put them to good use and now you'll have another pretty plant to talk to."

She laughed. "I don't talk to my plants."

"Oh, really? My ma always did and her plants grew like a jungle," he said smiling into her beautiful blue eyes.

Somehow he kept his gaze away from her pretty mouth. Until Sofia had moved to Echo, Travis hadn't been attracted to another woman after his wife, Jenny, had deserted him and his daughter, Pauline. Thanks to Marvin, he'd found out that Jenny had been cheating on him since before he and Jenny had gotten married.

Jenny had gotten pregnant by Sam Watson, Echo's former pastor, and she'd married Travis in a hurry to pass Pauline off as Travis' child. Travis hadn't known any of this until Marvin had interceded and told him to ask Jenny about it. After the explosion of heartache that had ripped his life apart, he'd waited for a year after Jenny had gone before filing for a divorce. Since he couldn't find Jenny and it was clear that she never intended to come home, the judge had granted him the divorce.

Pauline had been just as devastated as Travis, and she'd been worried that he wouldn't want her anymore since she wasn't Travis' biological daughter. However, in Travis' eyes, Pauline was his and always would be. Together, father and daughter had weathered the horrible situation, although there had been a period during which Travis had drunk heavily. But he'd gotten his act together for Pauline's sake so he could be the father she needed him to be.

That had been four years ago and it hadn't been until this past February that Travis had felt ready to possibly pursue a relationship with a woman again. He'd known Sofia for those four years, but she'd also recently been betrayed by her significant other and hadn't been any more interested in seeing anyone than he'd been. The shards of their hearts hadn't been sufficiently healed at the time.

But over the summer when he and Sofia had often been around each other socially since they shared many of the same friends, he'd found himself thinking about her a lot. He'd begun looking forward to seeing her and talking to her. When Lucky had told him that Sofia had been approached by a couple of men, Travis had had to make a decision to either stay silent or pursue the lovely blonde.

Around early October, he'd begun making excuses to drop by the Hanover House while she was working. He also knew what time she normally went to the store in the morning. He made sure to go to Temples' store around that time a couple of mornings a week and casually "run into" her. After a month of this, he'd finally gotten up the nerve to ask her to dinner. He was just waiting for her acceptance.

Sofia smiled. "I've heard people say that it helps, but I've never done it."

"The trick is naming them so they know which one you're talking to. At least that's what Ma used to say," Travis said.

"What's a good name for a fern?" she asked, looking the plant over.

"Fern?" Travis suggested with a chuckle.

She rolled her eyes a little, but smiled. "I knew you were going to say something like that."

"Lola," Travis said.

"Lola?"

Travis winked at her. "She's a saucy fern."

Sofia laughed. "A saucy fern? Now I've heard it all."

"That's right. Well, I better let you get back to work and I have to get back before the warden comes lookin' for me," Travis said. "Have a good day."

"Wait a moment," she said. "Does your invitation to dinner still stand?"

Travis kept his demeanor calm even though his heart lurched. "It sure does. What night is ok for you?"

Sofia felt a little funny about going the same night she was supposed to have gone with Zeb, so she said, "Thursday?"

"Sure. That works," he said. "Around six-thirty?"

"That'll be fine," she replied.

"I look forward to it, Miss Sofia," he said, touching the brim of his black hat before leaving the kitchen.

Sofia smiled as she watched him walk back to his horse. She liked his rolling, loose stride and broad shoulders. He was a little over six feet tall with long, sandy-brown hair and rich, coffee-brown eyes. His easy smile was hard to resist and she liked his sense of humor.

He rode off and she went to check on her ham, anticipation for Thursday filling her. Then she felt badly for being happy about going out with Travis. Shaking it off, she told herself she had nothing to feel guilty about. She wasn't committed to either man and, after her disastrous relationship with Gary, she was going to enjoy having two men vie for her affections.

Sofia knew that she would have to eventually choose one or the other, but for now, she deserved to have some fun after closing herself off from the possibility of romance for so long. Feeling better, she went about her work with a clear conscience.

"That's the look of a happy man."

Travis groaned as he carried a hay bale from the barn to the pasture. "What do you want, Earnest?"

Marvin smiled, unperturbed by his attitude. "Well, I came to give you your Thanksgiving bonus, but it you don't want it—"

Travis snatched the check from his fingers, folded it, and put it his jeans pocket. "Thanks, boss."

"That was rude," Marvin said. "No matter. What's making you smile so? Could it be a certain Miss Carter?"

Travis cut the binder twine around the bale and started spreading the hay out along the fence line. Then he cupped his hands around his mouth and called his horses. He didn't just shout for them, however. He let out a loud whinny that sounded just like a horse.

Marvin had heard Travis do this a thousand times, but he always enjoyed it. Travis loved horses so much that he spoke their language and often controlled them by horse-speak alone. An answering whinny sounded over the rise that hid the rest of the pasture from view. A beautiful palomino mare cantered towards him, followed by eight other mares and fillies.

Travis whinnied again and smiled as more of the "ladies," as he called them, sped towards them. He slipped through the fence as they arrived, petting them as he nickered at them. Not only was it a good way to socialize with them, he was able to look them over and make sure none of them had any cuts or other ailments.

The horses began eating the hay and Travis came out of the pasture. Marvin looked over the horses, and although in the past he hadn't been able to tell a good horse from a bad one, he'd learned some things from

Travis. The horses before them were sleek and strong and Marvin knew that they were a much better quality than in the past. Letting Travis have free rein of the horse operation had been a great decision on Marvin's part and it was paying off.

"They're certainly looking well, Travis. Well done," Marvin said, patting a filly who wanted some attention. He loved animals and enjoyed petting the horses and other animals on the ranch.

"Thanks," Travis said. There was a time when it had been rare to receive praise from Marvin, but over the years, he'd softened, showing his appreciation for all of Travis' hard work. "I want to talk to you later on about a stallion I want to buy, but I gotta get some other stuff done."

Marvin chuckled. "Is that your way of avoiding my enquiry about Sofia?"

Travis knew that Marvin wasn't going to let it go. "I'm taking her to dinner at Mama T.'s on Thursday night."

Marvin's eyes lit up. "Splendid! Do you have a nice suit? You need to get a haircut. Go see Win. You'll want to take her some flowers, of course."

Travis frowned. "It's just dinner."

With an eye roll, Marvin said, "You couldn't be more wrong. This is the first time you're taking her out and you want it to be memorable so that she wants to see you again. Not only that, but as I understand it, Captain Rawlins is also interested in her. You have competition, Travis, so you have to make a strong impression on her."

"Zeb asked her out?" Travis asked. "I didn't know."

"Well, aren't you glad I asked you about her?" Marvin's expression was smug. "What would you do without me?"

Travis shook his head. "You're the strangest friend I've ever had. I used to hate you. You have no idea how much. But it got so I could tolerate you and then I actually liked you. But you need me, too."

"You're absolutely right, and may I just say that I'm very glad that we're friends now," Marvin said. "Now, about that suit and flowers. I can help you with both of those."

Travis thought about it. His suit was old and out of style. If Zeb was interested in Sofia, too, he needed to outdo the captain and secure her affections. He smiled at Marvin's eager, expectant expression. "All right. You can help me. I wanna show her that I have another side."

"Excellent!" Marvin said. "Finish up what work you need to this morning, but we'll leave at noon for Dickensville to go see my tailor. You'll need to be properly fitted. By the time Thursday comes, you'll look so handsome that her heart will flutter. I'll come to the barn at noon. See you then."

Travis grinned as Marvin walked away. As complicated as Marvin could be, he was also fun in his own way. As he continued with his work, Travis grew even more excited about Thursday and kept smiling. He hadn't been out with a woman since Jenny and he was finally in a place where he could look forward to it. Travis felt a happiness that had been missing for a long time. Determination to sway Sofia in his direction filled him and he planned to do whatever he could to make that happen.

Chapter Four

A couple of days after his accident, Zeb felt well enough to be up and around. As long as he walked slowly, he was able to keep the dizziness at bay. His pain had diminished somewhat and he had a little more strength. It was time to begin doling out Skyhawk and Dog Star's punishment.

Slowly, he walked upstairs to their room, knocking on the door.

Dog Star opened it. "Hi, Captain. Come in."

Zeb stepped inside their room and looked around at the decorations on their walls. A couple of dream catchers adorned spaces above their beds, and colorful woven blankets covered their beds. Judging from the books on their beds, they'd been doing homework. He was glad to see it.

"Good afternoon, gentleman," he said.

Skyhawk had been lying on his stomach, but he sat up now. "You're out of bed. That's a good sign."

"Yes. It's slow going, but at least I'm up and about. And so now begins your punishment," he said, smiling.

Skyhawk folded his arms over his chest in a defiant gesture. "What kind of punishment?"

"Starting tomorrow, we'll be up at five-thirty sharp every morning except Sunday. I have something in store for you," he said.

"Five-thirty?" Dog Star's frown was comical.

Zeb said, "Yes. I thought braves were up early to hunt."

"We are. We're gonna miss hunting with Wild Wind," Dog Star said.

Zeb took that into consideration. "Ok. Monday, Wednesday, and Friday you're mine. The other days you may hunt. But I get you after school and on Saturdays, too."

Skyhawk's expression darkened further. "What are you going do to us? I just want to be prepared."

"I'm not going to *do* anything to you. You're going to help me with some things," Zeb said. "You'll see. I like your room, by the way. Did you make the dream catchers?"

"No. Mrs. Emerson made them," Dog Star said, speaking of their teacher.

Zeb frowned a little at her mention. The woman avoided him like the plague and while he could understand the Cheyenne woman's aversion, it bothered him. "She does very nice work. They remind me of the one given to me by a woman in Chief Dull Knife's tribe."

Skyhawk's eyes rounded. "You met him?"

Zeb nodded without thinking and had to close his eyes against the dizziness that followed.

Dog Star wasn't sure whether he should touch Zeb, but he didn't want him to fall down. He took his arm and guided him to a chair. "Sit here before you fall over."

Zeb sat down and opened his eyes once his head stopped spinning.

Skyhawk leaned towards Zeb. "What was he like? Were you fighting him? Did he kill soldiers? Did he wound you?"

"Easy, Skyhawk," Zeb said. "I met him shortly after he escaped from the military in 1879. I was stationed at the Sioux Reservation in Nebraska, when Chief Red Cloud granted him shelter with his tribe."

"What was he like?" Dog Star asked.

This was Zeb's chance to make inroads with the two troublemakers and he was going to take it. "As you can imagine, I was in awe of the man who'd led his people with such distinction and bravery. He was an intelligent, thoughtful, inspiring man. He only wanted to take his people home again, but the army considered his band renegades, which I found ridiculous. It's wonderful that his people were finally allowed to return to their tribal lands, but it's terribly sad that he didn't live to go with them."

Skyhawk gave him a dubious look. "You liked him? You like Indians?"

"Skyhawk, are there white people whom you like?" Zeb asked.

"Well, yeah." He smiled. "I like Mrs. Taft. She's a lot of fun. And the McIntyres are out friends, too."

Edna Taft had been hired as the school's part-time house-mother and she was popular with the kids.

Zeb smiled. "Yes, she is. If you like certain white people, why does it surprise you that I like Indians?"

"Because you're the army," Dog Star replied.

Zeb leaned back against his chair. "Contrary to popular belief, there are many army soldiers who actually like Indians. Unfortunately, they're vastly outnumbered by those who don't like them. I'm one of those who'd prefer to be friendly with them."

"Have you ever killed any Indians?" Skyhawk asked.

Zeb met his dark gaze. "Yes, I did. But to be fair, they were shooting at me," he said, wryly. "I've never killed innocent women and children, though."

Skyhawk nodded, respecting Zeb for telling the truth. He thought Zeb seemed very different out of his uniform. It was nice having a conversation where he wasn't reprimanding them for misbehavior.

Zeb rubbed his forehead. "I think it's time for me to go lie down again for a while." He slowly rose from his chair. Dog Star anxiously watched him, ready to steady him. "I'd be happy to have you come tonight at seven to hear some war stories."

Dog Star asked, "Will you tell us more about Dull Knife?"

"If you want," Zeb said.

A smile flashed across Skyhawk's face. "We want."

"Ok. I'll see you then."

Zeb cautiously walked from the room, almost ramming into Mrs.

Singing Lark Emerson. Instinct made him reach out to steady her, but it made him dizzy and she had to make sure he didn't fall instead.

"My apologies, Mrs. Emerson," he said. "I didn't know you were there."

Her dark eyes filled with concern. "You shouldn't be roaming around like this."

Zeb frowned at her scolding. "I just wanted to talk to the boys a moment. I'm going to lie down now."

"I'll help you," she said.

"I'll be fine."

"Yes, you'll be just fine when you fall down the stairs and finish killing yourself," she said.

"Fine. I don't have the energy to argue right now," he said.

They started down the stairs. Zeb held onto the banister and put his other arm around her shoulders. Under normal circumstances he wouldn't have been so familiar with her person, but it couldn't be helped at the moment.

She guided him down the stairs, through the kitchen to the doorway that opened into the back hallway leading to Zeb and Cade's separate quarters.

"I can take it from here," he said. "Thank you for your assistance, Mrs. Emerson."

"I'll make sure you get there," she said.

Zeb barely held back a retort. He stopped at his door. "Again, thank you. Have a pleasant evening," he said, taking his arm from around her.

She faced him, looking into his eyes, and her defiant expression reminded him of Skyhawk's. "I wasn't eavesdropping, but I heard you tell Skyhawk and Dog Star that you met Dull Knife."

"Yes, I did." Her lips pursed and he suddenly noticed how soft they looked. "Why does that irritate you?" he asked.

"It doesn't. You do," she blurted. Her eyes widened.

Ordinarily, he would have taken offense and snapped back at her. Instead, he laughed, leaning back against the wall.

Lark, as her friends called her, was disconcerted by his actions. She'd expected him to be angry over her sarcastic comment. His warm and infectious laugh was in sharp contrast with his normally stiff demeanor. A smile tugged at the corners of her mouth.

Zeb straightened. "Yes, I'm aware of that. I seem to aggravate many people." He straightened and opened his door.

"Captain?" Lark fidgeted with her skirt a little, uncomfortable about what she was about to do.

"Yes?"

"This is forward of me, but I would like to hear some of your stories," she said.

One of his dark eyebrows rose. "You would?"

"Yes. Would you mind if I came with the boys to hear a few?"

He'd never thought that any of the children or Lark would want to hear his stories. It wasn't completely proper for her to be in his quarters, but Skyhawk and Dog Star would be present so they would have chaperones.

"No, I don't mind. I told them to come at seven," he said.

With the ghost of a smile, she said. "Ok. Thank you."

"You're welcome." He watched her go back down the hall, her long black braid swinging to and fro. "Well, how do you like that?" he mumbled, entering his rooms.

He lied down, pondering what had just happened, before nodding off.

When seven o'clock came, Zeb was glad that he'd changed into jeans and a buttoned-down shirt, because Lark was accompanied by all of the children. They filed into his parlor and seated themselves on the floor as he gave Lark a questioning look.

"It would be good for them to hear about a great chief from someone who has met Dull Knife," she said, her eyes pleading for his acquiescence. She'd put aside her pride for the sake of the kids.

Seeing all of the eager faces, Zeb couldn't deny the kids the opportunity to listen to his stories about some of their people. "I'd be happy to oblige."

He sat in a chair, trying to decide which story he would tell first. "I'm glad you all came to hear my stories. It's nice to have an audience."

Happy Turtle, a thirteen-year-old boy said, "Tell us about a battle, Captain."

Lark said, "Let Captain Rawlins decide what he would like to tell, Happy Turtle."

He frowned, but stayed silent.

Zeb smiled. "Actually, Happy Turtle, I *would* like to start with a battle, but it might be a slightly different story than you're after. I had just joined the army and I had dreams of fighting in fierce battles of all kinds and coming out the victor…"

For an hour and a half, Zeb told his stories. Indians especially value a good storyteller, since most of their history is handed down orally. Surprisingly, Zeb proved that he could spin a yarn quite well. Zeb enjoyed enthralling his audience as he told exciting, sad, and humorous accounts of his career. He related stories involving only the army along with ones that included Indians, making them laugh when he poked fun at his previous superiors.

Dog Star asked, "Did you fight all the tribes of Indians?"

"That would be almost impossible, Dog Star. There are far too many tribes for any one person to fight them all."

"How many are there?" Gray Dove, a seven-year-old girl asked.

"Hundreds, really."

"What ones did you fight?" Skyhawk asked.

"Cheyenne, Lakota, Comanche, Apache, Pawnee and Nez Perce," Zeb said. "But I didn't fight with all of them. I was also assigned to reservations and forts. You have to remember that I've been in the army for twenty-five years, so I've seen and done a lot."

"You must be old," said Jumper, a ten-year-old boy.

Zeb laughed. "I don't know about old, but I'm not exactly young anymore."

Lark saw that Zeb was losing steam; it was time to let him get some rest. She would help Ellie Benscotter, the house-mother, put the children to bed.

"It's time for bed, everyone," she said.

The children groaned in protest, but rose from the floor.

"Let's thank Captain Rawlins for such a wonderful evening," she said.

The kids expressed their appreciation to him as they filed out. Gray Dove trotted up to him and hugged him. It was the first time that one of the children had ever done that and he was deeply touched. He embraced her and patted her back.

"Goodnight," she said in her sweet, little voice before running out the door.

Zeb followed all of them to the door, thanking them for coming to see him. Lark hung back after the youngsters had gone.

"Thank you for sharing your stories. It meant a lot to them." She lowered her eyes. "And to me, too."

"You're welcome. I had a good time, too," he said.

"I'm glad. Well, goodnight."

"Goodnight," he said.

She left him then, but he didn't leave her mind as she assisted Ellie in getting the little ones dressed for bed and tucked in. She'd seen a completely different side of Zeb that night and was reminded that things were not always what they appeared to be. He'd dramatically recounted his exploits while leaving out the gory details since there'd been little children present.

His sense of humor had surprised her and she'd laughed as much as the kids had. Zeb was a handsome man to begin with, but his attractive smile and nice laugh made him even more appealing. The direction of her thoughts unnerved Lark, and she reined them in. She was at the school to work and help the children, not to think about men, especially army officers, no matter how handsome they might be.

Chapter Five

Sofia almost didn't recognize Travis when he showed up at her door Thursday night. His dapper appearance was a pleasant surprise. The gray suit with the black paisley vest had obviously been tailor-made and he wore fine black shoes, too. He'd gotten a haircut and he looked every inch a proper gentleman.

She smiled and said, "My goodness, Travis. Don't you look handsome? Come in."

Travis stepped just inside the door, taking in the way her blue sateen dress fit her hourglass figure to perfection. "Thanks. I just happened to have this lying around," he quipped, holding a small earthenware planter out to her. "I saw these sitting out on the street and they told me they were lonely. I thought you could give them some company."

She took the pot of geraniums from him. "If you keep this up, I'm going to have flowers up to the ceiling," she said. "Where did you get these at this time of year?"

"I don't know what you're talking about. I told you they found me outside," he said, smiling.

Sofia chuckled. "Ok, keep your secret."

Travis nodded. "I will. A man has to have a couple. Are you ready?"

"Yes."

He held his hand out for her heavy wrap and she gave it to him, thinking how nice it was to have a man who wasn't just a friend to that for her. Travis didn't just put it on her; he settled it nicely around her shoulders and then lightly squeezed her upper arms.

They left her apartment and he gave her his arm.

"You know, it's good for my ego to be escorting such a beautiful woman," Travis said.

"Thank you," she said. "It's nice to be escorted by a handsome gentleman, and I mean a real gentleman."

"What do you mean?"

Sofia said, "My ex-fiancé had no idea how to treat a woman. I'm not sure why I stayed with him when it became clear after a while that he didn't appreciate me. I defended him and I don't know why."

Travis harrumphed. "I'll tell you why; you get good at seeing only what you want to see. I understand what that's like."

"I'm sorry for being melancholy. I don't have any reason to be," she said.

Travis stopped walking and faced her. "Sofia, both of our hearts have been put through the wringer. I completely understand what you've been through, so it's ok with me to talk about it. I didn't want to at first, but when I finally did, it helped me."

Sofia shook her head a little. "I think it was so much worse for you. I wasn't married with children when I discovered Gary's infidelity."

"It was hell for a long time," Travis said. "But it got better. I've been more worried about Pauline than myself, but she's been so strong. She was only nine when everything went to heck. I can't believe she just turned thirteen."

They continued walking.

"She's such a pretty girl, Travis. She's also respectful and intelligent," Sofia said. "You have a wonderful daughter."

"Thanks. I think so," Travis said.

Arriving at Mama T.'s, Travis lightened the mood again by telling Sofia about some of his more humorous moments working for Marvin. Sofia relaxed, enjoying his company and the excellent food. While Travis still teased her, he also acted a little differently with her, flirting a little more openly than usual. It was nice to be paid that kind of attention and Sofia forgot all about Gary as the evening progressed.

His breath came out in loud pants as he carried his prey along the woodland trail. He hadn't expected the woman to put up such a fierce fight. She'd gotten in a few good hits before he'd subdued her. He'd thought that he might have to shoot her, but he'd succeeded in knocking her out before that had become necessary.

Although it would have been better to hold off a while longer, he hadn't been able to control his hunger any longer. So, when the opportunity had presented itself, he'd taken it, even though he hadn't properly planned everything out like normal. He would be very careful from this point forward, however.

Reaching the place where his horse was tied, he slung the woman over the saddle and tightly lashed her to it. He hurried along the path, the horse trailing behind him. It was a long time until he made it to his destination. The woman started waking up, so he held a chloroform-soaked rag over her face until her movements subsided again.

He led his horse into the old barn, and pulled the woman off the animal. Carrying her to a corner stall, he put her down on a pile of straw. He put shackles on her ankles and chained them to ring on the wall. He handcuffed her wrists, and then covered her with a few blankets to keep her warm. Brushing her long, brown hair back from her cheek, he thought her beautiful.

"Sleep, my beauty. You need your rest," he said quietly. "Because once it starts, it won't stop until what needs doing is done."

An ominous chuckle escaped him as he left the stall.

Arliss heard Andi gasp and was instantly alert. "What is it?"

She rolled over to face him as they lay in bed. "He's out there."

He looked out the window. "Who's out where?"

"No, not here," she said. "Out in the night somewhere."

Running a hand over her arm, Arliss felt her tremble. "Come here," he said, pulling her to him. "Take a breath and then tell me what you saw."

Since meeting Andi, he'd grown skilled in guiding Andi through times like this. If she purposely tried to have a vision or get an impression, she was fine, but when they came to her in a dream or out of the blue, it could be frightening for her.

Arliss' warmth and familiar scent helped calmed her. Andi closed her eyes, trying to recall every detail possible from the dream. Patiently, Arliss waited, knowing that it was important not to disturb her. She would speak when she was ready.

During these episodes, Arliss stayed firmly in control. Blake wasn't always patient if something truly disturbing came out. His instinct was to protect Andi, even though he had no power against a vision or dream. R.J. was better at dealing with them, but he, too, could be moved to anger. Arliss was able to control those feelings and project an air of calm around Andi, which enabled her to gather as much information as possible without being distracted.

Andi recounted the dream to Arliss, relaying everything from sight, sounds and smells to him. He refrained from asking questions until she said, "That's everything."

"Ok," he said, rubbing her back gently. "You never saw his face?"

"No. He was always in shadow, but I don't think he was quite as big as you. It seemed like he had trouble carrying the woman so far. He was very out of breath."

R.J. came forth after Arliss had sternly warned him to be patient. "Hello, love. Were you able to tell what he was wearing? Was there anything unique about his clothing?"

Andi closed her eyes again, willing her mind to go back into the dream. "He wore dark trousers and a gray sack coat with a scarf. No hat."

"Can you see the color of his hair?"

"Brown or blond. I don't know which, but it's not black."

R.J. asked, "How old did his voice sound?"

"He definitely wasn't a teenager, but he wasn't old. I don't really know."

"All right. Was it deep, raspy, cultured?"

Andi tried to hang on to it, but the dream was fading now and she groaned in frustration. "Somewhere in the middle."

"Easy, Andi," R.J. said. "It's all right. Do you think this has anything to do with those murdered women?"

Andi said, "I think so, but I can't be sure. I couldn't get a strong enough impression. It was faint. I need more contact, something more concrete."

"Such as?"

Andi wrapped her arms around herself protectively and R.J. pulled her close again.

"I need to go to where they were buried."

R.J. cleared his throat. "I'm not sure that's a good idea. You might become overwhe—"

"Come out, come out, wherever you are," Andi said, bringing forth Arliss. She only did this when it was important to talk to a certain personality. "Did you hear what I said to R.J.?"

"Yeah. Don't be mad at him, honey. He and Blake just can't help being protective like that. I am, too, but I think I understand better that we need to give you strength to do what you were born to do. If that's what you need to do, we'll get Evan in the morning and go out there."

"That's fine, but I need Shadow," she said.

"Shadow? Why do you need him?" he asked, surprised.

"I need his darkness. I need him to drag me down and he has darkness in spades."

This was the first time Andi had ever said such a thing to him. "Sort of like an anchor?"

She nodded. "Yes. I don't think I can do it by myself."

42

"We can't help you? We've killed people," Arliss said.

Caressing his cheek, she said, "Yes, but you've done it for the right reasons, I guess you'd say. There really isn't any true darkness in you."

He kissed her palm. "If that's what you need, then so be it. Now, try to get some sleep. You're gonna need it."

Andi snuggled against him and felt Blake come forth. "Don't try to talk me out of this," she said.

He sighed. "I won't. I know that you have to do it just like we have to do what we do. It's a part of what makes you, you. I just hate the thought of you being upset."

"I know," she said. "I'll be all right."

He nodded and kissed her temple. "Yeah. You're strong."

They fell silent and soon Andi slept. However, Blake stayed vigilant against danger even though the enemy was not the sort that he could fight.

"What do you want me to do?" Shadow asked as he, Evan, Arliss, and Andi stood in the woods the next morning.

"You don't have to do anything. I just need to hold your hands," she said.

Shadow smiled, his blue eyes shining in the dim light. It was sufficiently dark in the forest for him to leave his dark glasses off. "This is an odd date, don't you think?"

Andi laughed. "My husband is right over there."

Shadow let out a sarcastic snort. "I'm not worried about him."

Andi smiled and held out her hands to him. "Now, think dark thoughts. That's what I need, and don't let up until I tell you to."

"Are you sure about this?" Shadow asked. "I've never done anything like this, and I'm a little leery about it."

Evan said, "Shadow, Andi's experienced with this sort of thing. It'll be ok."

"Very well." He took Andi's outstretched hands.

Nausea gripped Andi immediately as the putrid stench of something rotten filled her nostrils. She almost gagged as she fought it down. Gripping Shadow's hands tighter, she allowed his darkness to pull her mind down until it seemed as though she sank right into the ground.

Women's screams reverberated inside her mind and she whimpered a little. Evan moved towards her and Shadow would have released her hands, but Arliss intervened.

"Shh! Let her work. Don't let go, Shadow. It's dangerous for her to just jump out like that. I'll know if she's in trouble," Arliss said quietly.

Andi heard them, but the screams were louder and held her attention. She tried to see their faces and then she felt like she was falling. The ground rose up and hit her, but she understood that it wasn't really her. It was a different woman and she was screaming.

"No! Stop! Please, stop! I'll do anything you want, but don't kill me. No one has to know!"

Her plea went unanswered by her abductor as he unbound her feet, but left her wrists tied together. He rolled her over onto her back, looping a rope around her ankle, and pulling it tight. She tried to kick, but a backhanded blow to her cheek subdued her long enough for him to get her other ankle tied down.

He had to wrestle her, but he succeeded in tethering each of her hands the same way. She lay with her limbs spread out in four directions.

"He tied her up," Andi said. "With her legs and arms spread out. She fought hard, but he managed it." She felt herself begin to lift out of the vision. "Shadow, darker thoughts."

Shadow frowned but complied with her request. Closing his eyes, he conjured the image of his cage, remembering what it had been like to live in it.

Andi sank back down and suddenly she was in the woman's body as she lay on the forest floor. *She felt stones and twigs dig into her back. Gazing up at the sky, she saw the stars above the circular opening in the trees. The clearing was filled with the sounds of crickets and somewhere an owl screeched in the trees.*

A tear rolled down Andi's face. "She knows she's going to die. There are stars out. She's in a clearing."

Arliss moved closer, but he didn't touch Andi. "Can you make out any constellations?"

"Yes. The Big Dipper and Orion. That's all I can see."

The man spoke close to her, making her gasp in surprise.

"I see you for what you really are. Others might disparage you and say that you're unclean and I guess if I was looking at you through their eyes, I might see you that way. But you're an instrument, and you should be honored to be chosen. Your unclean soul might not mean anything to anyone else, but it's infinitely important to me."

She felt him stroke her hair and flinched away.

Andi concentrated hard on his voice to see if it sounded familiar to her. "More, Shadow."

If it weren't so important, Shadow would have refused. However, he wanted to make sure Echo would be safe for the women about whom he cared to go about their lives without the fear that something would happen to them. He brought to mind the beatings he'd taken from his father.

These dark, turbulent thoughts transferred their wicked energy to Andi and she was able to hear the man better. His voice was vaguely familiar to her, but it wouldn't come to her.

"You'll be rewarded for your sacrifice," he said. "You'll see. Don't be afraid."

"No!" she shouted when he pushed her skirt up high on her leg.

"Hold still so it doesn't hurt so much," he said. "It won't take long."

The woman sobbed in dread. A knife cut into the tender flesh of her left thigh and she screamed. It was a different kind of torment than she'd been expecting. She raised her head to see his head bent at his task. She saw the small knife blade flash in the light of the lantern he'd sat near them.

"I don't understand. What are you doing?" she asked.

The vision dimmed as he raised his head to look at her.

"No!" Andi cried. "Not now! Shadow! All of it! Now!"

Shadow was sweating and trembling by this point, and he balked at going any further.

"SHADOW!" Andi screamed.

With a coarse growl, Shadow delved deeper into the muck that had been his life at one time, dredging up the very worst of the worst. Both he and Andi went down on their knees. Evan moved to interrupt them, but Arliss stopped him.

"Don't. If you pull her out right now, I don't know what'll happen. Let her finish."

Evan's face was set in grim lines. "I know you're worried about your wife, and so am I, but there's Shadow to think about, too. Who knows what he's remembering. I don't want him to snap."

Arliss put a hand on Evan's shoulder. "I know, but she'll take care of Shadow. It'll be ok. Trust me."

Evan pursed his lips and nodded reluctantly.

Andi tried desperately to pull every last ounce of energy from Shadow, but he was faltering under the strain and she couldn't sustain the vision. She floated up and saw a cage in which a teenaged boy sat on a scummy mattress. He looked at her with heartbreaking sadness in his beautiful blue eyes and she knew that he was Shadow.

Giving him a smile, she reached out a hand to him, urging him to take it. When his fingers closed around hers, she pulled him out of the cage, rising up to the surface with him in tow. Opening her eyes, she saw Shadow's bent head and his sweat-soaked hair. His body shook and his hard grip on her hands was painful.

"Shadow," she said softly, her voice tremulous. "Open your eyes. No more cages. No more pain. You have to open your heart to the light. Let your soul free."

Shadow opened his eyes as a rough sob escaped him. He let go of her hands and rose unsteadily to his feet. "You've seen how deep down it is. The light will travel only so far. Don't ask this of me again."

He stumbled away, barely remembering to put on his glasses before breaking out into the cold sunshine.

Chapter Six

After Shadow left, Andi gathered her wits and told Evan every detail of her vision. He wrote it all down in his notepad to be cross-referenced with what already existed in the case file back at the sheriff's office. Most sheriffs wouldn't have given Andi's abilities any credence, but Evan had seen her work first hand on several occasions, so he believed the things she told him to be factual.

"Could you tell how recent this was?" he asked.

"No. I'm sorry I wasn't able to get more information for you. Poor Shadow. I shouldn't have asked him to do that. I owe him a huge apology."

Evan said, "You couldn't have known that would happen. Don't approach him for a while, though. I'll make sure he's all right."

They were interrupted by Thad, who called out to them. His tone of voice told Evan that something was very wrong.

"Over here," Evan said.

Thad jogged through the vegetation to them. "We can't find Molly. She left real early this morning to go to the paper. Keith was still sleeping. She left a note. He stopped by the *Express* on his way to work at the cobbler shop, but she wasn't there. No one has seen her."

They were surprised to see Marvin following Thad.

"He's been helping look," Thad said, by way of explanation. "We even went back home, thinking she might have gone back there. Killer can't get a fix on her because she's left too many trails here and there in town, so that's useless."

"Oh, no," Andi said. "What if the woman I saw was Molly? I have no idea who she was. I never saw her face."

"What are you talking about?" Thad said. "What woman?"

Andi and Evan explained the situation to them.

Marvin said, "That's why Shadow merely growled at me as he passed me. He went into the Burgundy House, most likely for a drink to steady his nerves. Are you strong enough to continue, Andi?"

She nodded. "But I need help. I need—"

"Darkness," Marvin said. A malicious smile curved his mouth. "If it's darkness you want, I can supply plenty of it. You just happened to pick the wrong brother. Shadow's childhood isn't something he likes to deal with in a way, but I approach things from a different angle."

He gave her his hands, and Andi hesitated to touch him. She could feel waves of it coming off him. Would it be too much for her? There was no time for fear. Molly's life depended on it. Grabbing his hands, Andi let Marvin's evil thoughts drag her back down.

The shivering of her body woke Molly. Even with the blankets covering her, she was cold. Her head hurt and her body ached. She moved to sit up, but the shackles on her legs and wrists made difficult. Looking at the handcuffs on her wrists, she tried to remember what had happened.

She'd been on her way into town to work on the printing press. Not wanting the next printing to be delayed, she'd decided to leave early so she could get it done sooner. One minute she'd been on her horse and the next, someone had dropped out of tree, landing on her and knocking her off her horse.

Molly wasn't like other women in that she was skilled with guns and knives. She was tough and had put up a good fight. However, she'd forgotten to put her knife on that morning and when she'd gone for the gun that was tucked into her boot, her attacker had smothered her face with a sweet-smelling cloth. She'd fought him off, but the drug had made her dizzy, slowing down her reaction time.

He'd come back at her, hitting her hard in the face, and knocking her down. She'd grabbed a handful of dirt, thrown it in his face, and tried to run. Although he'd been partially blinded, he'd managed to catch the back of her coat, hauling her back against him. Roughly, he'd covered her face with the cloth again.

Molly had tried not to breathe, but her lungs had finally screamed for oxygen. When she'd pulled in a huge gulp of air, the chloroform had instantly disabled her, and she'd gone down. The last thing she remembered was being trussed up and lifted onto her horse.

Sunlight seeped in through the cracks between the boards of the barn and she saw that she lie in a stall. Molly's first instinct was to scream for help, but if she did that, he'd know she was awake, which would cut down on her time to figure out how to escape.

What would Thad do in a situation like this? The famous bounty hunter was known for his ability to get out of tight spots and she'd read some of his accounts of past adventures. She assessed her situation. Her ankle shackles were chained to a ring attached to the stall. Her hands were handcuffed, but at least they were in front of her. The stall door was closed, but she didn't know if it was locked.

Take one thing at a time. You have to get free first. As quietly as she could, Molly got to her feet. If he was near the barn and heard her chains rattle, it would draw his attention. She shuffled over to where the leg shackles were fixed to the wall. Maybe she could get it loose.

And then what? He'll still hear the chains, and it's all you can do to walk like this, let alone run.

She examined her handcuffs. Could she pick them, thereby freeing her hands, so she could work on the shackles? She wasn't wearing any pins in her hair and without her knife, she had no tool to use on the locks.

There has to be something in here. Looking around, her eyes caught sight of a nail protruding from one of the wooden walls. It looked like a water bucket had been hung on it at one time. If she could free the nail, it might work on the handcuffs.

Resting her hands on her stomach, she muttered, "Don't you worry. They're gonna find us, but in the meantime, I'm gonna do everything I can to get us out of this."

By her calculations, Molly was four months along. She'd only told Keith the week before and they'd decided to keep it a secret until the baby quickened in case something happened again. She'd miscarried three years ago and they'd been afraid of it happening again. They were cautiously optimistic about her carrying to full-term this time.

She forced herself to stay as calm as possible, knowing that the stress wasn't good for the baby. She probably shouldn't have fought so hard earlier that morning, but her only thought had been to get away from the man.

Going over to the nail, she tugged on it, dismayed to find out that it was firmly embedded in the board. Gripping it with the fingers of both hands, Molly wiggled the nail hard, encouraged when she felt some give in it. Keeping an eye open for her kidnapper, Molly went to work on the nail in earnest.

<hr />

"Keith, I wanna find her as much as you do, but you have to calm down," Thad said as Keith paced back and forth in the sheriff's office.

"This lunatic could have her anywhere!" Keith's big fists clenched as he thought of his wife being in the clutches of an evil maniac. He grasped Thad's biceps and looked down at his father-in-law from his six foot-five height. "She's pregnant, Thad. Molly is pregnant."

Thad's dark eyes met Keith's unflinchingly and he grinned. "Congratulations, Keith."

His determination to find the young woman who'd become a daughter to him doubled. He couldn't blame Keith for being worked up. Who wouldn't be in his shoes?

Thad said, "We're gonna find her—them. No matter what it takes, we'll find them. I just had an idea! Killer might not be able to track Molly, but he might be able to pick up her horse's trail. C'mon. We have to go back home."

Keith trusted Thad's instincts, knowing that the man had captured some of the sneakiest criminals. His hopes rose as he and Thad rode for the McIntyre residence.

Shadow downed his fourth shot, hoping that it would steady his nerves enough, so that he could ride home. He tried to quell the tremors coursing through his body, but he wasn't having much success. Someone put a hand on his shoulder and he whirled around, striking out.

Marvin staggered back from the brutal blow to his chest that knocked his breath from him in a big *whoosh*. He went down on his knees grabbing a chair to keep from falling completely to the floor.

"Marvin!" Shadow knelt next to his twin.

Marvin's face reddened and he clutched his chest, his eyes bugging out. Finally, he was able to take in air again.

Relieved, Shadow said, "I'm so sorry. I didn't know it was you. Are you all right?"

Marvin nodded. Shadow helped him onto his feet and guided him over to a barstool. Sitting down, Marvin just concentrated on breathing for a couple of minutes while Shadow sat watching him anxiously.

Marvin cleared his throat. "I know you're angry at me, but I didn't think you wanted to kill me," he rasped.

Shadow's jaw clenched. "I don't want to kill you. If I did, I would have done it long ago."

Marvin chuckled as he rubbed his chest. "This I know. It's just a good thing it wasn't Andi or someone weaker than me. They'd be dead or passed out at the very least."

The release of pent up emotion had settled Shadow down and his tremors had almost completely subsided. "I'm angry, but not at you anymore, Marvy. Evan pointed some things out to me that made sense and I think he's right."

"And what were these things?" Marvin asked before drinking Shadow's shot of whiskey that still sat on the bar.

"One being that I've never really given much thought about what you went through back then. You've never talked to me about, so I assumed that you were all right. But the fact that you talked to Thad about it all and showed him my cage tells me that you were almost as affected by it all as me," Shadow said.

Marvin sighed. "I always felt that I had to be so strong because you had been treated infinitely worse than me. What you suffered ... well, we won't go into that, but I don't pretend to know what that was like. What I suffered was a complete identity crisis. I didn't know who I was anymore. The only thing I knew was that you were my brother and that I needed to help you."

Shadow said, "It wasn't fair for you to have it all rest on your shoulders, Marvin."

"The whole thing wasn't fair to either of us, yet it happened," Marvin said. "Before you say it or even think it, there's nothing I would have done differently regarding you. Nothing. You must realize something, Shadow; I did it as much for myself as I did you."

"I don't follow."

Marvin stared into Shadow's eyes. "You're my brother, the one person outside of Ronni and Bree whom I know I can count on, no matter what. We might argue and fight from time to time, but when it comes right down to it, neither of us could ever walk away from the other. I needed you as much as you needed me. It's that simple."

Shadow nodded. "You're so right. I'm just sorry that I didn't realize that you were still hurting from it all."

Marvin laughed. "I didn't realize it, either, until I told the whole sordid, horrific story to Ronni and then bawled like a baby in her arms. It wasn't until then that I knew that it wasn't entirely behind me."

Shadow said, "I did the same thing with Bree, so don't feel bad." He snickered. "Does it bother you that your once-upon-a-time sworn enemy is somewhat responsible for all of our happiness?"

"There just went all of my goodwill towards you," Marvin said, giving Shadow a scathing look.

"I'll take that as a yes."

Marvin pursed his lips. "So what was this other kernel of wisdom that Evan passed on to you?"

"That it's time to take down the cage."

Marvin's hand tightened around the shot glass and his jaw worked. His cold fury seeped into Shadow's mind. "I've been telling you that for the past several years, but you wouldn't hear of it. Any time I brought it up, you refused to discuss it. Suddenly, Evan says the same thing and you're willing to do it?"

"Don't be jealous, Marvin. I only seriously considered because Evan made me that it's the right thing to do for you, too. Just like you did things for me, I want to do this for you, too," Shadow said.

Marvin sighed as his anger abated. "You're right. Petty jealousy doesn't become me. I suppose I should be glad that you're ready to do it no matter how it came about."

"He said he'll help us do it and take it to Bernie's junkyard."

Marvin threw up his hands. "Why not make it a party and be done with it? We'll invite everyone over to dismantle it and then have a banquet afterwards!"

Shadow laughed at Marvin's sarcasm. "I don't know about doing that, but ..." Shadow's eyebrows drew together. "You're a genius."

"I am?"

"Yes. We really should do something like that. A celebration dinner of sorts," Shadow said. "To sort of permanently remove the specter of ... evil? I'm not sure that's accurate, but you get my meaning."

A smile spread across Marvin's face. "How splendidly morbid. We'll talk about it with the girls tonight. Now, I see that you're feeling better. I know it was rough going with Andi."

Shadow looked up at the ceiling. "Yes. I'll never do that again. I can't. I haven't truly thought about it for a couple of years. It's always lurking inside, but actively putting myself there again in my mind is too hard. I hate to say that, but it's true."

"Don't feel badly, Shadow. I helped Andi. She didn't get much more because she was too tired right now. I also came to get you. We have to go help look for Molly. She's missing," Marvin said.

Shadow stood up. "Why didn't you tell me? We've been sitting here all this time!"

"Shadow, I've been thinking about the situation the whole time. Running about without any sort of plan won't solve anything. All of the usual and the unusual places have been searched and she's not there," Marvin said. "She's my friend and believe me, I'll do anything to find her, including calmly thinking up possibilities. Now, since you know the woods around here like the back of your hand, do you know of any deserted properties? A place where one might wish to hide with a kidnap victim?"

Shadow nodded. "Yes. Let's go."

Chapter Seven

Oblivious to the dramatic events elsewhere, Travis went about his work that morning, thinking about Sofia as he cleaned stalls and groomed horses. Their dinner last night had been a success, and he smiled as he thought about her acceptance to come for supper the next night. He also thought about the way she'd smelled and the softness of her cheek when he'd kissed it at the conclusion of the evening.

He hadn't gone to the store in the morning, figuring that he'd let things lie for a day. He didn't want to make her uncomfortable by smothering her. So he'd dropped Pauline off at school on his way through town and headed to work without stopping anywhere. This is why he hadn't heard about Molly. He liked Molly, who had made him see how much his heavy drinking had been hurting Pauline—and himself. She'd been instrumental in him giving up alcohol except for on special occasions.

Picking up a tool belt from in the tack room, Travis went outside to where his horse was tied. He'd just mounted when he heard Marvin call him.

"Out here, boss," he replied.

Marvin's black expression made the hair on Travis' arms stand up. "Come with me right now," Marvin said.

"Why? What's wrong? Is it Pauline?" Travis' heart thumped with fear.

"No. It's Molly. She's missing. We need every available man to look for her," Marvin said. "Shadow knows some abandoned farms. She might be at one of them. Evan is of like mind and has Billy helping him."

Travis rode into the barn and waited while Marvin and Shadow saddled fresh horses, letting the ones they'd been riding rest. Then they rode out, intent on finding their friend.

Molly finally managed to get the nail out of the stall wall. Her fingers were bloody and sore, but she'd done it. The need to save herself for her baby's sake had driven her on despite the pain. She was exhausted, and would have sat down to work on the handcuffs, but she didn't want to be at a disadvantage in case her captor showed up. She didn't know where he was, but she wasn't going to let her guard down.

Her hands trembled, and she dropped the nail. She retrieved it and took a few moments to steady her nerves before attempting to pick the handcuff locks. Something moved outside the stall, and she halted her work. A cat cried, and she relaxed before resuming her lock picking. No matter how hard she tried, she couldn't trip the release mechanism.

However, she decided to hang onto the nail since she might be able to use it as a weapon. She put it in the front pocket of her jeans just as footfalls neared the stall. Carefully, she moved as far away from the stall door as possible.

Molly jumped at the sudden appearance of a face over the stall door. She assumed that it was the same man who'd kidnapped her, but she couldn't be sure. He wore a gray cowboy hat, a silver masquerade ball mask, and a blue bandana. It all effectively hid his face, but she could see that he had blue eyes through the eye slits in the mask.

"You better let me out of here, mister," she said. "Because there's gonna be all kinds of people lookin' for me and you don't wanna meet up with any of them."

He cocked his head a little. "No one will ever find us where we are."

The high-pitched, girlish voice unnerved Molly. She'd been expecting a masculine voice and while she could still tell that it was a man, the falsetto voice scared her more than if he'd drawn a gun on her.

"I wouldn't be too sure about that," she said, somehow keeping her fear from showing.

He cackled and threw a flask and couple of eggs at her, which she ducked to avoid. The eggs cracked, but she saw that they were hardboiled.

"Enjoy your lunch, sweetie," he said with a feminine wave before leaving.

Molly stayed where she was for several minutes to make sure that he wasn't coming back. Slowly, she sank down onto the bed of straw. She picked up the flask, opened it, and sniffed. There was no odor. When she tipped it a little, water ran from it. She drank a swallow of it and recapped it, saving some for later.

Her stomach recoiled at the thought of food, but for the baby's sake, she peeled an egg and forced it down. Then she folded her arms on top of her knees and rested her head on them. She prayed as tears trickled from her eyes.

Evan and Billy walked through the woods with Billy's dog, Homer. After Andi had finished with her second attempt, Evan had quickly gone to get his friend and the dog. The coonhound was an excellent tracker and they'd put him on Molly's scent out on the road to Thad's house. Homer was a little quirky in that he would only comply with polite requests to do something.

He'd cast around on the road, where they'd found the signs of a scuffle, for a while before he'd barked once, indicating that he'd picked up something. The marks in the dirt weren't the sort that would be discernable unless they were looked for. Slowly they'd made their way through the dense undergrowth because the ground wasn't where Homer was finding Molly's scent. It was from bushes and trees.

Billy also kept an eye on the ground, finding boot prints here and there.

"These are deeper. He was carrying something heavy. If Homer is picking up Molly's scent up higher than the ground, the guy must be carrying her."

Evan agreed. "Yeah. So where's her horse? It didn't come home, and he obviously didn't use it to carry her."

"Maybe he killed it. That's what I'd do. A rider-less horse coming home is bound to tip someone off that something's wrong," Billy said.

Homer let out an excited yelp and pulled harder on his leash, letting them know that the trail was getting warmer. They walked faster through the forest until they came to a trail. Billy crouched down to look at the ground. It had recently been disturbed, but he made out a partial hoof print.

"He put her on a horse here," Billy said, rising. "They went right."

Homer concurred, pulling Billy in that direction. They continued on for a few minutes before Homer stopped and cast about again. He let out a whine and both Billy and Evan's stomachs dropped. Homer only whined like that when he lost a scent.

They walked further on, but Homer didn't pick the scent up again even though he smelled nearby trees and bushes. Finally, he sat down in a dejected pose.

Billy knelt by Homer and hugged him. "Don't feel bad, buddy. You did a good job. You got us this far." He took out a piece of wasna and gave it to him. "What do you want to do, Sheriff?"

"Let's keep going down this trail. Maybe we're on the right track," Evan said. "Just keep your eyes peeled."

"Right," Billy said, leading Homer forward.

Something crashed through the undergrowth about twenty feet to their left and Homer growled and bayed loudly. Both Evan and Billy raised their guns in that direction, ready to fire. A big horse burst out onto the trail and charged them. Evan fired a warning shot, and the horse neighed. More gunfire rang out, and Billy and Evan dove for cover. Billy dropped Homer's leash and the dog went after the horse at first, but then bowed in a playful pose.

"Knock it off, Homer!" Billy whispered at him.

They heard the horse stop and whicker.

"This is Sheriff Taft! You better put down your weapon and come out here with your hands up!" Evan shouted.

They heard a bunch of swearing and recognized Thad's voice. Getting up, Billy and Evan walked out onto the trail at the same time Thad and Keith rode their horses out of the woods.

"I didn't hit either of you, did I?" Thad asked, looking them over.

"No," Evan said. "What are you doing?"

"Well, Killer couldn't pick up Molly's scent, but he picked up Prince's and led us through the woods," Thad said. "Then we ran into you guys."

Billy said, "Homer tracked her here. The reason Killer didn't pick up on it was because the guy was carrying Molly. Homer got her scent from trees and bushes that she must have brushed against. He lost the scent right about here."

Keith said, "He couldn't have just disappeared into thin air."

Billy shook his head. "He didn't. He put her on a horse and headed that way." He pointed past where Thad and Keith sat on their horses. "We were gonna keep going until you guys showed up and shot at us."

"To be fair, you guys shot first," Thad said. "I was just protecting Killer."

"All right," Evan said. "We don't need to argue about that. Let's keep going."

Keith had already moved out, but Thad hung back. "This is bad enough for all of us, but especially him. Molly's pregnant."

"Oh, no," Billy said. "I mean, that's great, but this isn't good for her and the baby, and I can understand why it would make him even more determined to find her."

"Yeah." Thad dismounted. "You guys take my horse. I'll ride Killer."

The stallion came when Thad whistled for him. Thad tapped on his shoulder and Killer knelt so that Thad could mount and then rose again.

"You go ahead and ride, Evan. I don't want to let go of Homer," Billy said. "I'll follow along."

Evan nodded and swung into the saddle of Thad's horse. The riders trotted off with Billy and Homer bringing up the rear.

As he rode along, Keith's urgency to find Molly consumed him. She was his soulmate and he couldn't lose her. They were looking forward to this baby, too. Ever since he'd met her, she'd brought him happiness and he would do whatever it took to get her back. He wanted to gallop along, but he kept a level head.

Rushing headlong into danger wouldn't help Molly, and he didn't want to tip off her captor that they were coming. Not only did he want to rescue his wife, but he also wanted to catch the miscreant, so that Echo was safe again for women.

All four men were of the same mind, and kept alert for any sign of danger. They didn't encounter any trouble as they moved along the trail. Homer and Killer didn't pick up any trace of Molly, but that didn't mean that she hadn't been taken that way. Presently, the trail opened up onto a large meadow next to a farm.

They halted, looking the place over, watching for any signs of life. There was no movement, so they slowly rode across the meadow to the house. It was in terrible shape, with cracked windows and broken porch floorboards. The porch roof sagged, and the front door hung by only one hinge.

Billy took Homer all around the building, but there was no sign of Molly. When he came back to the others, he said, "I looked in some of the windows and I didn't see her. It doesn't look like anyone's been using the place, either."

Keith said, "I'll check the barn."

"I'll go with you," Evan said.

They rode over to the barn, with Billy and Homer following, but the barn was empty and there was no sign of Molly.

Keith swore. "He had to bring her this way! This where the trail leads, but he must have continued on somewhere."

Billy said, "I'll run around the property with Homer and see if he can find her trail."

Evan and Keith rejoined the rest of the search party, waiting as Billy and Homer were performing their task.

Killer suddenly let out a blasting whinny and spun around. Three riders emerged from the trail Evan's party had just come from.

"Aw, jeez," Thad said. "Who invited the Unholy Bookends?"

Travis and the Earnests rode up to them.

"Gentlemen," Marvin said. "I see that we're crashing the party."

Evan said, "Yeah. Killer and Homer trailed Molly here, but they lost the scent now."

Shadow said, "We've been looking at the abandoned farms around here. There are three more that I know of."

Homer let out a long howl, signaling that he'd found the trail again. They rode over to Billy and the dog.

"It starts again right here," Billy said, pointing to a break in the foliage that was the entrance to another trail.

Evan drew his gun and started his horse down the trail. "You take care of Homer, Billy. No talking as we go through here, men. Let Homer work. We don't wanna become moving targets, either. Stay sharp."

"Evan, stop!" Billy shouted. "Don't move!"

Evan reined his horse to a halt, and Billy handed Homer's leash to Keith. Billy crawled over the trail to a spot just in front of Evan. "Back up," he said and then looked around.

He found a long branch and tore it off a tree. Cautiously, he swept the trail with it. They all jumped when a bear trap sprung, its cruel, metal teeth snapping the branch in half. Homer barked at the trap.

Billy said, "We must be on the right track. I'll bet this trail is booby-trapped the whole way through. We're gonna have to move slowly."

"Damn," Evan said. "That would have got my horse or you, Billy. I'm glad you saw it. Thanks."

"You're welcome," Billy said.

He collected some more branches and started sweeping the trail from side to side. Their going was very slow, but safe, thanks to Billy's keen tracking eyes. He snapped more bear traps and even found a couple of

Apache foot traps. These were mostly used for game, but would do great damage to a human calf or horse leg.

Marvin was curious and saw how deadly the trap could be as Billy explained it to him.

"So my leg would go through the false covering, but when I tried to pull free, these sharpened sticks would skewer my leg?"

"Right," Billy said. "You'd have two choices; stay put and hope someone friendly found you or rip your leg up in order to get loose."

He pulled the sharpened sticks from the side of the hole, and he threw them off into the woods so that no one who might come upon the hole would be hurt if they stepped into it. The trail grew steeper and Homer started baying steadily. They were nearing their quarry.

Chapter Eight

Molly had given in to her exhaustion after her abductor hadn't returned. She'd sunk down on the straw and closed her eyes. She dreamt of a little girl who looked like Keith. The brown-haired girl ran along a country path, followed by a dog. As they ran, the dog started barking loudly.

Jerking awake, Molly realized that the barking was real and stood up stiffly. She tried to see out the slits between the boards on the outside wall of her stall, but couldn't see anything. The dog kept barking and it sounded like a hound. She hoped that someone was with the dog.

Taking a risk that the dog belonged to the man holding her, she began screaming. "Help! Help me! In the barn! I'm in the barn!"

The dog quieted.

"No! Don't go away! Help me! Please help me!" She pounded on the boards as she shouted.

"Molly? Molly!"

Keith!

"Yes! I'm in here!"

"We're coming!"

A minute later, the big barn door was shoved open.

"Over here!" Molly said.

Keith ran to the stall, threw open the door, and took her in his arms. "It's ok, honey. I'm here. You're safe. We're gonna get you out of here."

She nodded as she wept against his chest. "I'm s-sorry. I didn't mean for this to happen."

Keith stroked her hair as he held tears in check. "I know, honey. It's not your fault. It's ok now. Let's go home."

"You have to get these off me," she said.

Looking down, Keith saw her metal bound hands and ankles. "You're in your bare feet. And your hands are bleeding."

Molly nodded. "That's from digging out a nail."

Thad came into the stall. "There you are. Always causin' trouble." He hugged her, kissing the side of her head. "Are you hurt?"

"Just my fingers and my feet are freezing. I can't really feel them."

"Let's get you out of these handcuffs," Thad said.

Keith looked at the metal plate that the leg shackles where attached to and frowned. His urgency to get his wife home overrode common sense. Grasping the chain close to the metal plate, he used his mighty muscles to rip it right out of the board.

"Well, that was impressive," Thad said, smiling. "But I think we'll just use this." He held up a handcuff key.

Keith looked at it. "Oh."

The rest of the rescue party had gathered around the stall and they laughed at Keith's chagrined expression. Thad unlocked Molly's handcuffs and then chose a different key from the ring he carried. Bending down, he released the shackles, and Keith picked Molly up. Evan stepped forward, wrapping a blanket from his bedroll on his saddle around her blue-cold feet. Billy took of his coat and laid it over her. Evan rolled up the blankets that had already been in the stall to keep as evidence. He might even be able to put Homer on the scent of whoever they belonged to.

"Thanks, everyone," Keith said. "Let's get you home."

All of the men greeted Molly as he carried her past them out of the barn.

Evan followed them, stopping Keith. "Molly, I'll keep this brief for now. Did you get a look at him?"

She shook her head. "No. I fought him like hell, though. I probably shouldn't have because of—" She broke off quickly, looking at Keith.

"It's ok. They know about the baby," he said.

Evan smiled. "We're all really happy for you kids."

"Thanks," Molly said. "I never saw his face. He was here around noon, but he was wearing a gray Stetson and he covered his face with a bandana and a party mask of some sort." She shuddered. "If that wasn't bad enough, he talked to me in this real high voice, like a woman. That was the scariest part for me. He threw me a flask of water and a couple of hardboiled eggs for lunch. He hasn't been back since then."

Evan wrote what she told him down. "About how tall was he?"

"Maybe six feet tall? I don't think as tall as you, Evan," she said. "I think his hair was brown. Average build. If he wouldn't have knocked me out with chloroform, I'd have been able to get away from him. I had my boot gun and I'd have shot him. Damn! He has my boots and my gun!"

Keith said, "Don't worry about that right now. We'll get them back if we can."

Evan said, "Go on. I'll come over later tonight to talk to you, Molly."

She nodded. "I'll think on it. I know every detail helps."

Thad patted her arm. "That's my girl."

She smiled at him and then Keith gave Molly to Thad so he could mount. Keith took her back and settled her across his lap.

"Travis, Marvin, you go with them. The rest of us are gonna investigate this place," Evan said.

Marvin didn't argue, perfectly willing to escort the young couple safely home. Travis was also cooperative since law enforcement wasn't where his talents lie.

Once they'd gone back the way they'd come, Evan turned to the other three men. "Let's get to work, fellas."

After they helped see Molly and Keith home, Marvin and Travis returned to the Earnest ranch. Travis had a couple of things to finish up before he left for the day. He did them quickly, anxious to get home to Pauline. After seeing what had happened to Molly, he had a strong need to hug his girl. He felt so bad about Molly's ordeal and for the fear her family had gone through.

He'd stopped by the Hanover House to ask Sofia if she'd take a raincheck after the day he'd had. She'd been very understanding and they'd made plans for another night. Arriving home, he found Pauline starting supper.

"Hi, Peanut," he said, embracing her tightly.

She hugged him back. "Did they find Molly?" News of the missing reporter had quickly spread around town.

"Yeah, we found her. There was a bunch of us looking for her. She'll be fine," Travis said. "You make sure you don't walk anywhere alone and I don't want you out after dark, ok?"

She nodded against his chest. "Don't worry, I won't go out. I don't wanna get taken."

He kissed the top of her head. "That's my good girl." Releasing her, he asked, "What are you making?"

"Fried chicken and mashed potatoes."

"Mmm. That sounds great," Travis said and told her that Sofia wouldn't be coming over that night.

Pauline was both relieved and disappointed. Her feelings regarding her father seeing a woman were muddled.

Travis was proud of Pauline's growing knowledge in domestic things. She helped keep their house clean and often started supper. He couldn't believe she was thirteen. They finished cooking and sat down to eat.

Pauline ate a few bites of food before asking, "Pa, are you gonna see Miss Carter a lot?"

"I'd like to. How do you feel about that?"

Her dark brown eyes lowered. "I don't know. What if you want to marry her?"

"Well, we're not thinking about that right now. We're getting to know each other better. But, what if I did?" he asked.

"Would she want me? I'm not hers."

Travis put a hand over hers. "Honey, I promise that I would never marry anyone who didn't like you or want you in her life. You're my girl and you come first. All right?"

She nodded.

"Besides, you like Sofia. You know what a nice lady she is," Travis said.

"I know, but it might be different since you're courting her," Pauline replied. "I do like her, but I don't want her to stop liking me. You might get married and she'll want a baby. And if she has a baby, what about me?"

Travis squeezed her hand a little. "Honey, if we did get married and have a baby, you would be a great big sister. That's what would happen. You wouldn't be left out at all. I promise you that, too. I wouldn't let that happen and Sofia's not that kind of person."

Pauline couldn't help feeling apprehensive about her father seeing a woman after the fiasco with her mother. She'd loved Jenny so much and to not only find out that her mother had been having a long-time affair with the former pastor and then to be abandoned by Jenny, had crushed her. Not to mention that she'd found out that she wasn't Travis' biological daughter.

The idea of Travis having a baby with someone else made her anxious. What if he decided that he'd rather have a child who was his and not her? Would he put her in an orphanage? Pauline tried not to think like that, but it was hard not to.

She bowed her head to hide the tears in her eyes. It was hard to swallow the bite of mashed potatoes around the lump in her throat. Finally, she managed it, but she couldn't eat anymore. She tried to hold back the tears, but they wouldn't stop.

Travis' hand closed around her upper arm and he pulled her to him, sitting her on his lap.

"Hey, listen to me," he said. "I love you so much and no one is ever gonna come between us. Do you hear me?"

She looked into his eyes. "But what if you don't wanna be my pa anymore?"

His brow knitted. "Why would I ever want to stop bein' your pa?"

"Because I'm not yours," she said.

"Not mine? Of course you are. Any man can sire a child, but that doesn't make them a father, Pauline," he said. "You're my daughter. I loved you before you were born and I was here when you were. And when I held you for the first time, I cried because I was so happy you were here. It makes no difference to me. I'm your father, and I always will be. It don't matter how old you get, I'll always be your pa. Don't you forget that. You hear me?"

She put her arms around his neck and he hugged her close. "I love you, Pa. I don't wanna lose you."

"You'll never lose me. I promise."

Her father's strong arms around her were comforting and she felt better.

"Now that we got that straight, how about you eat your supper?"

"Ok," Pauline said, returning to her chair.

She wasn't really hungry anymore, but she ate for Travis' sake.

"How was school today?" he asked, wanting to distract her by discussing pleasant things.

Pauline smiled and told him about some of the more amusing things that had happened. They were still talking about them when they cleaned up and went to the parlor. Travis challenged her to a game of checkers and that was how they passed their evening until her bedtime. He was glad that she was once again laughing and teasing him.

After she went to bed, Travis sat in his chair looking at a women's fashion catalogue. Pauline's birthday was next month and she'd let it slip that she wanted a new dress for good. This wasn't something he normally would have looked at, but there was no one else to do it.

He lowered the magazine. Wasn't there? A smile curved his mouth. He'd take the magazine to Sofia in the morning and ask for her help. It would be a good excuse to see her, and it really would help him out. Laying the magazine aside, he stood and stretched. He decided to go to bed since he had nothing pressing to do.

When he lie down, he looked over at the empty side of the bed and felt a cold loneliness embrace him. Thinking about Sofia, he could imagine being married to her. He remembered Marvin saying that Captain Rawlins was interested in her. Jealousy made him frown and he became determined to capture her heart and hopefully give her his heart in the process.

"You're a good man, Zeb, but I'm gonna give you a run for your money," Travis said.

Chapter Nine

Dog Star's arms trembled as he completed another pushup. He was on number thirty out of fifty, which wouldn't have been much trouble, but with a twenty pound flour sack on his back, it made it much more difficult. This was part of his and Skyhawk's punishment. Four mornings a week, they were subjected to exercise and calisthenics and Zeb didn't take pity on them. He'd only given them beginners' exercises, but the boys weren't used to these types of physical activities and their bodies weren't conditioned for them.

Cade did them with them to show them how because Zeb wasn't quite up to performing them. Normally, Zeb kept a rigid physical regimen, however, and once he was completely well, he'd go back to it.

Dog Star looked to his right where Cade was doing his pushups. The corporal's rhythm was rapid, smooth, and seemingly effortless. He, too, had a flour sack on his back—only his was fifty pounds instead of twenty. Dog Star's arm and back muscles burned as he pushed off again and sweat dripped from his forehead onto the ground.

Skyhawk wasn't faring much better, but his stubborn, defiant nature wouldn't let him give up. He wanted to prove to Zeb that he could take anything he could dish out.

"C'mon, men! Get moving! You're not done yet. Time's wasting," Zeb said sharply.

Dog Star said, "I'm trying! I'm dying!"

Zeb laughed. "If you think this is bad, just wait until you see what I have in store for you next."

Dog Star groaned in dismay.

Skyhawk grew angry and channeled it into the energy to complete the required number of pushups. He grunted as he rose again. His biceps were on fire, but he refused to succumb to the pain. A war song sounded in his head, and he used it to give him the strength to go on. He started singing it out loud.

Dog Star smiled and picked it up. They didn't know it, but Zeb grinned as he walked behind them, checking their form to see if he needed to make adjustments. He noticed the way they picked up speed, rising at the same time, and moving with the beat of the song. He often did the same kind of thing, losing himself in the song. It made the exercise go quicker and actually helped him perform better.

The boys reached fifty and stopped, sagging down on the ground while panting.

"We did it," Dog Star said. "And I'm still alive, thank the Great Spirit."

Zeb chuckled and took the flour sacks off their backs. "Good job, gentlemen. Get up now."

The boys did, their chests still rising and falling rapidly.

"Now, run to Wild Wind's place and back here in fifteen minutes," Zeb said, getting out his watch.

"What?" Dog Star asked. "Fifteen minutes? You know how far that is."

Zeb said, "Yes, I do know. It can be done. You like running around at night well enough. Now you're going to run during the day. On the count of three. One, two, three!"

The boys took off, sprinting out to the road and disappearing around a bend.

Cade was still working on his pushups. He usually did a hundred and he was almost there. Zeb watched him and itched to do them, too. When Cade finished, he shrugged the flour sack off his back and stood up.

"You know that they're not gonna make it back in fifteen minutes, don't you?" he asked Zeb.

"Of course I do," Zeb said. "But it'll give them something to strive for. Skyhawk especially will rise to the challenge just to prove he can. Dog Star will follow right along. Give it two weeks, maybe a little less, and they'll be conditioned enough to do it. I've done this before, Corporal."

Cade smiled. "Ok. You know best. I'm off to do some running of my own. See you after a bit."

"All right," Zeb said.

Cade jogged away in his old trousers and long-sleeved undershirt and Zeb longed to go with him. They often ran together and he missed it. Sighing, he went back to his quarters, but there was nothing there for him to occupy himself with. At loose ends, he wondered out to the large parlor and found Edna sitting in a chair, knitting while Gray Dove lay on the sofa sleeping.

Zeb frowned as he sat down. "Why isn't she in school?"

"She wasn't feeling well at breakfast and has a fever," Edna said.

"Oh. Poor thing. She's such a sweet child," Zeb said. "She hugged me the night I told stories."

Edna chuckled. "There's nothing like affection from children to make your heart a little warmer. You'd know if you'd taken the time to have a family."

Zeb gave her a sharp look. "You're one to talk."

Edna's eyebrows rose. "Excuse me?"

"Forgive me for saying so, but your husband passed away a long time ago. Why haven't you remarried?" Zeb asked.

"Because there's no man who can compare to my Rebel, that's why," Edna said.

Zeb said, "Have you ever given any man a chance?"

"You haven't given a woman a chance," Edna said. "Or maybe you haven't given yourself a chance to really consider it."

"Well, I'm remedying that. I was supposed to go out with Sofia the other night, but then I almost cracked my head open and had to postpone it. I'm going to see her later today and reschedule," Zeb said.

Through the grapevine of her friends, Edna had heard about the dinner date. "Well, it's about time."

Not about to be outdone, he said, "It's about time for you, too. You're doing much better, from what I understand, and you're full of vim and vinegar from what I can see. You're a beautiful woman. I'm sure you could have your pick of many men."

"I don't want to see anyone."

"What about Spike? He's a nice-looking gent and he's a good man."

Edna smiled. "Listen to you matchmaking. Spike and I are just friends. I have none of those sorts of feelings for him."

"All right. What about Rob Hastings?"

"Will you stop?" Edna said, laughing. "I don't have romantic feelings about anyone."

"Well, that's a shame. You have a lot to offer a man," Zeb said.

Edna shook her head.

Zeb said, "It's all right for you to meddle in my love life. Well, the love life I'm trying to have, anyway. But you don't want to take your own advice?"

Edna's blue eyes cooled a shade. "I think we'd best quit this discussion, Zeb."

He smiled at her hard tone. "Spoken like a true lawman's wife. Very well, but I think we know where each other stands."

"Yes, we do."

Gray Dove woke up and yawned. Spotting Zeb, she rose and, dragging her quilt with her, made her way over to him. She held her arms up to him. Smiling, he picked her up and settled her on his lap.

Draping the quilt over them, he said, "Were you lonely over there?" He felt her forehead and frowned at how warm it was.

She nodded and snuggled against him, quickly falling asleep. Zeb held her and found his eyelids growing heavy. He finally gave up, leaned his head back against the armchair, closing his eyes.

Edna smiled at the two of them, thinking how sweet a sight they made together. It surprised her how casually Zeb had picked up Gray Dove, as though he did it all the time. Gray Dove's sudden attachment to the captain was also surprising. There must be something about him that drew her to him, Edna surmised. Whatever it was, Edna thought that it was good for the both of them.

As she continued knitting, she thought about Zeb's taunt about her not giving another man a chance. She knew that he was essentially calling her a coward, and she'd never considered herself cowardly. Just the opposite, but his remarks had hit a sore spot. She'd thought about finding another mate a couple of times, but then she'd rejected the idea because her heart still belonged to her husband. Shaking her head a little, she thrust her musings aside and resumed her knitting.

He was still furious over Molly's rescue. He'd needed her and now she was gone. He should've known better. Once he'd heard who she was, he'd known he'd made a mistake. Of course they'd have hunted hard for her. She was the stepdaughter of one of the town deputies.

"That's what happens when you don't do your homework," he said to himself as he paced in his small kitchen. "You messed up and now you're gonna have to wait a little while again and find another target." His voice was high-pitched. In his normal voice, he said, "I need to find someone that no one will care about."

It had been so much easier with the others because they'd had no one to worry about them. Prostitutes were the perfect choice for that reason, but there were no more in Echo that he knew of. He knew that his kills had been found, but he wasn't overly concerned about that because he no longer needed them. They'd given their lives to his cause. After that, they were useless to him.

"You let your impatience get the best of you, and now they're more determined to find you," said the high-pitched voice. He shook his head. In his normal voice, he replied, "I need to complete the task. That's the only way it works. Then she'll be mine. The Master will give her to me. I just need one more."

He needed seven lives, the last one being very special. He was going to have to wait until closer to time to collect his next victim. He put on his black hat and left. He knew better than to wear the other one because someone might recognize it. Once his horse was saddled, he headed for town to find the perfect sacrifice.

Chapter Ten

S ofia was doing dishes when Travis stopped by to see her. He opened the front door at the Hanover House and smiled when he heard her pretty singing.

"Knock, knock," he called out as he walked back the hallway to the kitchen. Entering it, he smiled at her, admiring her beauty. "Good morning."

"Good morning, Travis. How are you?"

"Good, thanks." He picked up a towel and started drying dishes.

"You don't have to do that," Sofia said.

"I don't mind. I might as well be helpful while we talk."

His serious expression told her that he had something on his mind.

"What about?" she asked.

"Pauline. She's worried that if I get serious about someone, that the woman won't want her around. She's also worried that if I married someone and had a baby with her that she would be left out of the picture," Travis said. "I know that you're not that sort of person, but I have to make it clear that I'll never let anyone come between Pauline and me. I love my daughter and I'll always do what's best for her. I just wanted to get that out in the open."

Sofia approved of Travis' devotion to Pauline. "You are such a good father and she's a lovely young lady. I would never dream of trying to come between you. Anyone would be lucky to have Pauline in their life."

Travis nodded. "Thanks. I just had to say that on the record, so to speak. Now, I have something else to say."

Sofia washed the last dish and dried her hands. "All right. I'm listening."

Travis gathered his thoughts as he dried the dish. "I know that Zeb asked you out, too. I'm not the sort of man who will share a woman, so you'll have to make a decision pretty quick. I'm going to plead my case. I'm serious about you, Sofia. I don't know about love yet, but I like you very much and I think about you a lot. You're a good woman and so beautiful.

"I think we're compatible and we want the same things; a family and a happy home. You know that I want more kids. I always have. I'm a good provider with a secure job. With Zeb being in the military, he has to go wherever they tell him to. It's possible that you'd be picking up and moving often, or that if you stayed, he would still go and you wouldn't see him much. I don't know if he wants children, but if you did have them, they might grow up not knowing him much. He didn't want this post, so he'd probably jump at the chance to go somewhere else.

"Zeb's a good man, but he can't give you what I can; stability. I love Echo and I'm not going anywhere. I don't want to uproot Pauline, either. All of her friends are here and Adam has really turned the school around. You have family here and if you had to follow Zeb elsewhere, you wouldn't get to see them often." He took her hand and gave it a squeeze. "I'm not pressuring you, but I'd like to officially court you. I just thought you should know where I stand."

Sofia was impressed by his straightforwardness. "Thank you, Travis. It's good to know how you feel about me and I appreciate you being so forthcoming. I like you, too, and I agree that we're compatible. May I think about it?"

"Sure. Like I said, I'm not trying to be pushy," he said, smiling. "Well,

I'll get out of your hair. I better get to work." He kissed her cheek. "Have a good day."

"You, too," Sofia said, looking in his eyes.

Travis gave her a parting smile and left.

Sofia put a hand to her cheek and smiled. Travis had shown her more consideration in the past few weeks than Gary ever had during their entire relationship. When she compared the two men, they were like night and day. She thought about the qualities Travis had outlined about himself as she dusted. He was right about her looking for stability and having a family to love.

She hadn't spent much time with Zeb, so she felt it was a little unfair to make a decision, but the fact that he was a military man did give her pause for thought. Moving all the time would be stressful, and she wanted a husband who actually lived with her, not one who just came home here and there. She'd always wanted children and she didn't know if Zeb did, since he was some years older than Travis.

Sofia decided to reserve judgement until she went out with Zeb once and had him answer these sorts of questions. She would go to see him that afternoon to see how he was doing and to set up a time to go to dinner. Then she could make an informed decision. However, as she went about her duties that day, her thoughts were mainly on the handsome ranch foreman with the coffee-brown eyes and easy smile.

At lunchtime, Lark looked for Gray Dove and was surprised to find her sleeping on Zeb's lap. Even more surprising was that Zeb also slept. They looked so cozy together that Lark hated to wake them. However, she wanted to check Gray Dove's fever and try to get her to eat some soup.

She took a few moments to look Zeb over. His black hair was slightly tousled from resting his head against the chair and it gave him a boyish appearance. However, there was nothing boyish about his chiseled features and square jaw. She'd seen him exercising in the mornings wearing trousers and a long-sleeved undershirt, and she knew that powerful muscles lie underneath the uniform he wore most of the time.

Suddenly, she yearned to kiss him and grew angry with herself for thinking such a thing. Going over to them, she gently shook Zeb, keeping her touch brief. He opened his eyes and gave her a sleepy look.

"It's time for lunch," she said.

His eyes widened as he looked at Gray Dove. "We've been here that long? Good Lord. I never sleep like that."

Lark couldn't help smiling. "You've never had a severe concussion before."

Zeb's eyes followed the movement of her sensual mouth before he smiled back. "No. That's true." Looking at Gray Dove, he noticed that her hair looked damp. "I think her fever broke. Maybe my body heat helped sweat it out of her."

Lark felt the little girl's forehead. Although it was clammy, it felt cooler than it had that morning. "I think you're right. I'll take her upstairs and change her clothes. I don't want her to get a chill from having sweaty clothes on."

She took away the quilt and, as Zeb passed a hand over Gray Dove's back, he felt that her dress was indeed damp. "Yes, she's very sweaty. Gray Dove, time to get up."

The girl raised her head and looked into his eyes. "I don't wanna."

He smiled. "I know, but you need to have your clothes changed and eat something."

Lark said, "Come with me, little one."

The teacher tried to take Gray Dove's hand, but she wound her little arms around Zeb's neck and hung on.

"No. I wanna stay with *Ného'e*," she announced.

Zeb's gaze collided with Lark's, shock registering on his face. She was just as surprised as he was. Not only because Gray Dove had called him father in Cheyenne, but because Zeb had obviously understood the word. How much Cheyenne did he know?

Lark said, "Gray Dove, Captain Rawlins isn't your father."

"No, I'm not," Zeb said kindly. "But I'm honored that you would say that."

Gray Dove gave him an intense look, her little jaw stubbornly set. "You are if I say you are."

He arched an eyebrow and looked at Lark for help. Where had Gray Dove gotten such an idea? Lark's eyes twinkled and he saw that she was trying not to smile. He scowled at her.

He tried again. "I'm sorry, but I'm not. I'm your friend, but not your daddy."

Gray Dove embraced him again. "Yes, you are. You're *ného'éehe* and I love you." She sniffed, and Zeb felt her sob against him.

His own eyes grew moist and he didn't have the heart to correct her right then. "Shh. Don't cry. We need to get you changed, Gray Dove."

He rose with her and followed Lark upstairs to the room that Gray Dove shared with Dewdrop. Taking her in, he bent down, and tried to get Gray Dove to release him.

"You have to let me go now," he said softly.

"No! I don't want you to go," Gray Dove said.

She had a strong hold on him and he didn't want to hurt her.

"I'll wait right outside and we'll go down to lunch together, ok?" he asked.

Gray Dove put her feet on the floor and loosened her arms. "You promise?"

He stroked her hair. "I promise."

"All right," Gray Dove said.

Zeb stepped out into the hallway and Lark closed the door. He paced, trying to figure out what he was going to do about the situation. He didn't know how to dissuade Gray Dove's notion that he was now her father. He wasn't in any position to take on a child since he wasn't married. Who would take care of her when he had to work? What if he was transferred somewhere? Finding childcare might be difficult and he couldn't keep—.

"What am I thinking? I think hitting my head addled my brain more than I realized," Zeb muttered. "You can't take her and that's that."

In a few minutes, Lark opened the door, and Gray Dove hurried out to him, with a smile on her adorable face. He couldn't resist smiling back at her as she put her hand in his.

"Are you feeling better?" he asked her.

"Yep. I'm hungry. C'mon, *Ného'e.*" She tugged on his hand.

Lark barely suppressed a laugh as he passed a hand over his face and sighed, but she noticed that he didn't correct Gray Dove. Of course, the girl had already made up her mind and she didn't care if they said otherwise.

Zeb opened his mouth to object, took another look at Gray Dove's sweet face, and shut it again. With a resigned expression, he walked with her to the stairs. Lark looked on, thinking that once again the little Cheyenne girl and the handsome captain made a sweet picture together. Could the Great Spirit be at work there? Lark didn't rule anything out regarding the Creator. She followed them down the stairs, grinning the whole time.

Spike, the owner of his self-named saloon, looked at the two men who both sat with their forearms folded on top of the bar, their foreheads resting on their forearms. Both had short, black hair, and if they'd both been wearing brown sack coats, he'd have had a hard time telling them apart by looking at them from that angle.

However, he knew that Evan was the one in the sack coat and Zeb wore the navy blue wool one. When Evan sat like that, it meant that he was concentrating intently on a crime. Spike suspected that Zeb had something equally disturbing on his mind, since he sat in the same pose.

Zeb raised his head slowly, opening his eyes. He signaled Spike for another shot.

"What's eatin' you?" Spike asked him, giving him his drink.

"I suddenly seemed to have acquired a Cheyenne daughter," Zeb said. "I'm not her father, but she is insisting that I am, and I don't have the heart to keep correcting her."

Spike said, "Start at the beginning."

Zeb downed his shot and told Spike his story. "So I don't know how to handle the situation at all. I can't keep letting her think she's right, but how do I tell her without breaking her heart?"

A snort of laughter sounded from his left and he looked in Evan's direction. The sheriff had been deep in thought, but Zeb's story had gotten through to him, and it struck him as humorous.

"I'm glad you find this funny, Sheriff Taft. What would you do in my situation?"

Evan sat erect and cleared his throat. "So, she just started this out of the blue?"

"Yes. Until the night I told stories about my experiences in military, especially the ones about Dull Knife, I really hadn't much contact with the kids. Well, except for my two worst troublemakers."

"So what happened that night besides you putting everyone to sleep?" Evan gave Zeb a sarcastic smile.

"Actually, they enjoyed my stories so much that they didn't want to go to bed, smart ass. When the evening was over, Gray Dove gave me a goodnight hug," Zeb said.

Evan said, "Did she keep paying you more attention?"

"No—well, come to think of it, I guess she did."

"And did you respond to her?" Evan asked.

Zeb said, "Of course. I wasn't going to snub her."

"Mmm hmm. Does she pay that sort of attention to Cade?"

"No. I don't think so. He plays with all of the kids, though. Why didn't she gravitate towards him?" Zeb asked.

Evan said, "My guess is that she knows that you outrank Cade. I'm also guessing that she understands that you met with a great chief. She doesn't think of Cade as father material, more like an older brother, maybe. But, you seem more like a father to her. If no one else is around, you make the kids behave and you're sterner than Cade about it."

Zeb, "Those are good suppositions, Sheriff, but why wouldn't she feel that way about Wild Wind or Arrow? They're Cheyenne, her own people."

"I'll tell you why," Spike said. "It's a lot simpler than either of you think. She was sick and you held her while she was sick. That's something that usually a parent or grandparent does. Maybe some of that other stuff you said is true, Evan, but it's mostly because he took care of her."

"But, I didn't take care of her. She fell asleep on my lap and I fell asleep with her that way. I don't call that taking care of her," Zeb said. "I call that not doing my job."

Evan shook his head. "You've never spent time around kids before, have you?"

Zeb just gave him a sardonic look.

"My kids love taking a nap with me or Josie. Sometimes, they won't take a nap without one of us. Usually Josie does it since she's home during the day, but whenever I can, I do it. There's something real affectionate about doing that. I don't know how else to say it. At that age, they trust you to keep them safe and well, and they have complete faith in you."

Zeb smiled at the love in Evan's voice as he spoke about his children. "You're a pain in my neck, Evan, but you're a good father. Do you think that was all it took to convince her that I'm her new father?"

Evan shrugged. "It's hard to tell, but I wouldn't rule it out. Sometimes there's just no rhyme or reason to the way kids think."

"All of this is well and good, but it doesn't help me figure out what to do about it," Zeb said.

Spike said, "Yeah, that's tough. She's little and don't understand. They're hard to say no to at that age."

Zeb groaned. "You're not helping me."

"How the hell do I know what you should do? I've never had that happen to me," Spike snapped back.

Evan chuckled. "I don't think many men have. Maybe Wild Wind can help somehow."

"I'll ask him," Zeb said. "Well, gentlemen, thanks for the conversation and being absolutely no help to me at all."

"Anytime, Captain," Spike retorted. "Now pay up."

Zeb did and left the bar. He mounted his horse carefully, not moving too fast to keep from getting dizzy, since he'd had more to drink than he'd intended and the fact that he wasn't completely recovered. Looking up at the stars, he tried to come up with a solution for his dilemma.

Chapter Eleven

A few nights later, Skyhawk and Dog Star roamed through the woods after bedtime like usual. They never had any specific plan whenever they went out. Sometimes they observed deer without being noticed and came back in the morning to hunt them. Other times they practiced war dances they remembered under the stars and moon. It didn't matter to them what they did, mostly they roamed because of the sense of freedom they experienced being out alone without anyone to tell them what to do.

They walked along a deer trail, teasing each other about some of the girls they'd noticed looking at them that day, when they'd stopped in at the diner to see Boss.

"I saw her first," Dog Star said. When they were alone, they almost exclusively spoke in Cheyenne.

Skyhawk laughed. "So? She saw *me* first. She even winked at me."

"She did not!"

"Yes, she did."

Dog Star said, "It does not matter. We are not allowed to have anything to do with the girls in town."

Skyhawk said, "There is not much they can do about it once we are older, but I do not think that I want to marry a white woman. Maybe we will be allowed to go back to the reservation, so we can find wives."

Dog Star shook his head. "I doubt it. The whole point of taking us away from there is so that we learn to live among the whites. I think it is stupid because they do not want Indians marrying whites."

"Yes, but it is illegal for blacks and whites to marry. It is not for whites and Indians, or Indians and colored people, at least in Montana. I do not understand how these white people think."

"It is not just whites," Dog Star said. "It seems like each race only wants to stay with their own. Why cannot we all live in peace?"

Skyhawk snorted. "That will never happen. Are you saying you would marry a white woman?"

"Roxie is white and Wild Wind loves her. Arrow is married to Vanna and they are happy," Dog Star said.

Skyhawk threw a look at him. "Do you have a girl in mind?"

"No," Dog Star said a little too quickly.

"Yes, you do!" Skyhawk pushed Dog Star a little. "Who is it?"

"I do not," Dog Star said, pushing back.

Laughing, Skyhawk stumbled back a little. His right foot hit something, making him take another step back. As his left foot came down, his moccasin landed on what he thought was a rock—that was until he heard the sound of metal. The next moment he screamed as a wolf trap slammed shut around his ankle, the teeth digging deep into his flesh.

He fell to the ground and writhed in pain. "A trap! It's a trap!" he shouted.

Dog Star knelt. "Hold still. I'll get it off."

Skyhawk stopped his movement, but it was hard. He tried not to cry, but the immense pain caused tears to trickle from his eyes. Dog Star gripped the sides of the trap and pulled for all he was worth. They only budged a little. Then he remembered that traps couldn't be released that way. Lucky had shown them how to get one open.

"I am going to press down on the springs. You pull your foot out as soon as you can," he said.

Skyhawk said, "Yes."

Dog Star depressed the springs, using his weight along with his muscles to open the strong trap. Skyhawk forced himself to be patient as he felt the loosening of the trap. He didn't want to do anything to jar it out of Dog Star's grasp, making it snap shut it again.

"You should be able to get out now."

Skyhawk slowly pulled his foot away until he was clear. Dog Star cautiously let up on the springs and the trap closed again. He rushed to Skyhawk. "Can you get up if I help you?"

"Yes. I think so," Skyhawk said. He felt blood running down over his foot, soaking into his moccasin.

Dog Star got him up on his good foot. "Can you put weight on it at all?"

Skyhawk tried and groaned. "A little," he said.

Taking as much of his best friend's weight as he could, Dog Star helped Skyhawk to the field they'd walked through to get into the forest. Once they were out in the open, Skyhawk's shoulders sagged with dismay.

"I can't make it all the way home like this. You have to go get help," Skyhawk said.

"I am not leaving you here alone. The scent of your blood will bring coyotes or maybe even wolves," Dog Star said.

"You do not have a choice. You cannot get me home by yourself."

"We will wait here until dawn and then I'll go get help," Dog Star said.

Skyhawk said, "We will freeze if we do!"

Dog Star said, "I will build a fire."

Skyhawk shivered. "Fine, but then you go get help. Without blankets we will still freeze. A fire will keep any animals away."

Dog Star acquiesced and helped Skyhawk sit down. Quickly he gathered whatever sticks he could and some dry grass from the field. He was capable of making a fire without matches, but since he had some in the small pouch at his waist, he used them because they worked faster. Soon a small fire burned nicely.

Dog Star took stock of where they were, and he saw that they were closest to the sheep farm. He took off his coat and put it around Skyhawk. "I will be back very soon."

Skyhawk just nodded. Shock had set in, and all he cared about was the warmth of the fire as he shivered in front of it. Dog Star set out, streaking across the field.

Dog Star ran up on the porch of Win's cabin, which was closest to where he came across the meadow. The sheepdogs went after him until they recognized him. He jumped up onto the porch and pounded on the door. His lungs felt like they were filled with searing fire as he tried to catch his breath. He'd run faster than ever before, not giving in to the fatigue that had set in.

Win opened the door. "Dog Star. What is it?"

"Skyhawk …caught in trap …got him out …need help, can't walk," the boy replied, his words interspersed with pants.

"Ok. Hang on," Win said.

He turned around and had to fight to get past Sugar, who was trying to get out the door to see who had come by. She shoved her way out onto the porch and wanted Dog Star to scratch her ears. Dog Star didn't oblige, but he leaned on her for support while he caught his breath.

"Let's go," Win said, coming out onto the porch carrying a saddlebag.

They got a couple of horses from the barn and Dog Star led the way through the cold, starlit night.

Holding up his coat, which they'd found on the ground by the fire, Dog Star said, "He was right here. I gave him my coat and he was gonna wait by the fire for me. He can't walk, so he didn't wander off."

Win looked at the fire pit, in which burned sticks still smoldered. It looked like someone had put the fire out. "Where was the trap?"

Dog Star pointed to a copse of trees not far away. "We were walking on a trail in there and just messin' around. He stepped backwards and stepped right in the trap. I remembered how to release it, but it had big teeth and his ankle was really hurt."

"And you didn't see anyone around?"

"No, but I wasn't looking, either. I was too worried about Skyhawk," Dog Star said.

Win didn't know if the two things were related, but the story Billy had told about all of the various traps they'd found on the one trail during their search for Molly came back to him. All of the killer's victims had been women so far, but what if he was changing?

Looking at the woods, Win knew that they weren't going to be able to explore them until dawn. It was too risky to try to follow the trail in the dark. He ran a hand over his short-cropped, black hair. If Skyhawk had been taken by the killer, it would give him a big head start, and who knew what he'd do to the boy?

"You go home, Dog Star. I'm going to see Evan and we'll start searching at dawn," Win said.

"Dawn? We can't wait that long! We have to go now!" Dog Star gave Win a direct stare.

"I know you're worried about Skyhawk and so am I, but we can't track him in the dark, not with the possibility of more traps. We'll be able to—" He broke off, then said, "You go home and I'll get Shadow and bring him here. He can see in the dark almost like it's daylight."

The two of them mounted up and raced away.

Skyhawk came to suddenly, casting his gaze around. He lay on a cot in a shack. A small fire burned in a fireplace, and a table and two chairs sat off to the side. When he moved his legs to sit up, his injured ankle screamed with pain, and he groaned and stayed where he was.

"Hello?" he called out. "Hello! Is there anyone there?"

Silence met his inquiry. Gritting his teeth against the pain, Skyhawk sat up and pulled his left legging up. Tears sprang into his eyes at the sight of the jagged wound that still seeped blood. He put his legging back down and lay down again. The last thing he remembered was sitting by the little fire that Dog Star had built for him.

Who had brought him here and why? Maybe he'd passed out and they'd helped him. Maybe they didn't know who he was or where he belonged. He rejected that idea. He was an Indian boy and everyone around Echo knew that all the Indian kids lived at the school.

The shack door opened and a man came in. He wore a gray Stetson and a heavy black wool coat.

His blue eyes crinkled as he smiled at Skyhawk. "You're awake. That's a good sign. I brought some stuff so I can tend to that ankle of yours."

"Who are you?" Skyhawk was suspicious of the man.

"Corey March." He held out a hand to Skyhawk.

After giving Corey a measuring look, Skyhawk shook it. "How did I get here?"

"Well, I was on my way home from the Burgundy House and saw your fire. I stopped by to say howdy, but you were just lying there on the ground. You didn't wake up when I shook you. I looked you over and saw that you were hurt," Corey said.

"Why didn't you take me back to the Indian school? You have to know that I live there," Skyhawk said.

"Yeah, I figured that, but my place is closer than the school. You were so cold that I wanted to get you warmed up and bandage you up. I'm gonna take you home in the morning." Corey laid out some medical supplies. "But for now, it's important for you to stay warm."

Skyhawk couldn't fault his logic. Corey took off his coat, hung it on one of the chairs, and removed his hat. He looked to be somewhere in his twenties and his blond hair was a little disheveled.

"Ok, let's see to that ankle," he said.

He went over to the fire where a kettle hung over it. Corey poured some hot water into a basin that already had cold water in it. Bringing it over the table, he wet a cloth and wrung it out. He looked at Skyhawk with sympathy in his eyes.

"This is gonna hurt, but we need to clean your ankle and wrap it up."

Skyhawk nodded and braced himself. "Go ahead."

By the time Corey was done washing his ankle, sweat ran down Skyhawk's face. Corey put some carbolic acid on the wound and bandaged it. He gave Skyhawk a clean cloth to wipe his face off with. While he did that, Corey dipped a tin cup in a bucket of cold water and gave it to Skyhawk, who drank it down gratefully.

"I have some laudanum for you," Corey said. "That must hurt like a son of a gun."

Skyhawk nodded. "Yeah. Do you live here?"

"For now. I'm sort of working on something. Here you go," Corey said. "Take just a small swallow."

Taking the small bottle, Skyhawk hesitated to take the strong medicine. With everything going on around Echo, he was leery about the strange man. He'd been very nice, but that could change. The pain in his ankle made up his mind. He was tough, but he didn't know how much more he could stand. Following Corey's instructions, he took a sip and handed it back while he made a face from the terrible tasting concoction.

Corey chuckled. "I know it's not tasty, but it'll do the job."

"Why do you have all of this doctor stuff?"

"Well, it's just me up here and if I get hurt, I'm gonna need it until I can get to a doctor," Corey replied.

"Oh. That makes sense," Skyhawk said. The laudanum had started to work and his mind felt fuzzy. "I think I'll just lay down."

"That's it. Just rest until it's time to leave," Corey said.

Skyhawk smiled faintly and dropped into a heavy slumber.

Chapter Twelve

Shadow crouched by the bloody trap that Skyhawk had been caught in, scanning the trail in front of them. His keen night vision allowed him to see the path ahead very clearly. He didn't detect any unnatural disturbances in the leaves strewn over the trail. Other than the boys, it didn't seem as though anyone had been through there recently, but it also wasn't likely that that trap had been sitting there for months untouched.

He took a large branch and tapped the floor of the trail, but nothing happened. He stood up and walked forward as he swept the branch along in front of him. His concentration was so intense on his sweeping, that he didn't see the snare in front of his head until it passed over his vision.

His forward momentum caused the cable snare to tighten around his neck and bite into his flesh slightly. Stopping, he turned back towards Win.

"I seem to have been snared," he said, standing still.

He knew better than to struggle, instead finding the release mechanism, and letting himself out of the noose.

"Are you ok?" Win asked.

"Yes," Shadow said, moving to the side of the trail out around the snare.

He stepped on a metal trap pan and pulled his foot away quickly, but it still got his toes. He growled and then laughed at the pain and the ingenuity of whoever had set the trap. "Our trapper is a very devious fellow, Win. Don't come in here without sweeping it well. The idea is for the person who is snared to flail around and get caught in one of the other traps that I'm guessing are spaced to either side of the trail. It would surely doom them if they were alone, or if whomever was with them didn't have the proper tools to cut them loose."

Win said, "We have to get you out of that. I'll sweep all around there before I step up to you."

"Very well," Shadow said.

Win quickly performed the sweep, setting off two more traps. "This guy is as twisted as you are and an expert trapper besides."

Shadow chuckled as Win released him. "True."

"Let's get out of here," Win said. "Even with your night vision, it's not enough to catch everything. I say we bypass the trail and just follow the outside of the woods until we get close to a building. Then we'll have to sweep again. Boy, this guy's a real pain in the ass. I can't wait until he's caught and someone kills him."

Evan rode up to them as they emerged from the woods. Shadow had sent Marvin to alert him to the situation and then gone back home.

"Any luck?" he asked.

"Yes. Bad, I'm afraid. I almost hung myself on a snare and then I stepped into a trap," Shadow said. "Win just released me, but not for good behavior."

He sat down and pulled off his boot and sock. There were a few cuts on his toes, but they were intact. "Well, you don't have to start calling me Two Toes or something like that," he said, replacing his foot gear.

Evan smiled. "That's good." Then he sniffed. "Why do I smell perfume?"

Shadow laughed. "Rory decided last evening that she needed to do something about my smelly boots. So when our backs were turned, she got ahold of Bree's perfume and sprayed it in them. I have to admit that it worked even though it makes me smell like a woman."

Win and Evan laughed because they could well imagine their own daughters doing something like that. Win told Evan about their plan and Evan agreed with them. The three of them set off on their mission.

Corey jerked awake when someone knocked on the door of his shack. He hadn't been asleep very long. He got out of his bedroll and went to answer it. As soon as he unlocked it, the person on the other side slammed it open, and rushed through the door, shoving him back against the wall.

Anger-filled green eyes stared into his as a gun barrel was pressed into his forehead. Someone else came into the shack and Corey's eyes widened even further as he saw a man put on a pair of dark glasses while a Chinese man hurried over to the cot where Skyhawk lay.

"Wh-who are you?" Corey asked.

"I'm Sheriff Taft and these are my deputies. We've been lookin' for this boy. Who are you?"

"Corey March."

"Well, Mr. March, how did you get him?" Evan asked.

"I found him by a fire out in one of the fields on my way home," Corey said. "He was in a bad way, completely passed out. So I brought him home to take care of him until morning. I was gonna take him to the Indian school then."

"He won't wake up," Win said. "What did you do to him?"

Evan pressed the gun harder against Corey's forehead and he winced. "I gave him a sip of laudanum. He was hurtin' real bad. I cleaned his ankle and wrapped it up. That's all I did, I swear! I just wanted to help him."

Evan narrowed his eyes. "Help him into a grave?"

"What? No! Why would I want to kill some kid?"

"So you didn't kidnap him so you could carve up his thigh and slit his throat?" Evan asked.

Corey's face suffused with color. "No! What kind of man do you think I am?"

The shock on Corey's face convinced Evan that he was telling the truth. He lowered his gun and reholstered it. "Do you own this place?"

"Yeah, I bought it a couple of years ago, but I didn't come to work it until a few months ago. I've been saving up some money," Corey said, straightening his shirt.

Shadow and Evan exchanged looks. "A couple of years ago, huh?" Evan asked. "Turn around."

"What? Why?" Corey asked. "I didn't do anything."

Evan put his hand on his gun. "Turn around or I'll turn you around myself."

Corey complied and grunted as Evan put cuffs on him.

"You've been a real pain in neck with these traps," Evan said. "It was smart of you, I'll say that."

"Traps? What are you talking about? I don't use traps."

"Sure, you don't," Evan retorted. "Now, we're gonna go to the office and have us a nice conversation."

"What about? I didn't do anything with traps! I don't even know how to set one," Corey said.

"Then how come the trail here is lined with them?" Evan asked, spinning Corey back around.

"Trail? What trail? There's a trail?"

Shadow cocked his head a little. "The trail you used to get here."

"I've never used a trail. I use the road. Besides, if the trail is lined with traps, how could I get here carrying him? I put him over my horse and led it here," Corey said.

Shadow said, "He's right. That trail is too narrow to bring a horse through and he wouldn't have had enough time to set traps along the way."

Evan sighed. "Turn around."

Corey did, relieved when Evan took the cuffs off him. "Thanks. I swear I just was trying to help the boy. I don't even know his name. He didn't tell me before he passed out."

Win said, "His name is Skyhawk. We'd better get him back to the school so I can take care of him."

Shadow opened the door and Win was about to walk through the door carrying Skyhawk when a rifle blast rang out. Only Win's catlike reflexes saved him from being shot. He went down hard and Skyhawk bounced out of his arms. Evan dragged Skyhawk back from the door while Win scrambled farther into the cabin. Shadow slammed the door shut right before another shot rang out. The bullet splintered a board in the door and became embedded in the opposite wall.

"Get down," Evan said, pulling a petrified Corey to the floor with him.

Skyhawk roused and looked sleepily around at the men. With a lopsided smile, he asked, "Are we havin' a sleepover?"

Shadow grinned. "If we are, it's the worst sleepover in history."

The boy smiled again and then put his head on Win's arm. "Goodnight," he said.

Even though they were pinned down by an unknown enemy, it was still funny. What happened next wasn't however.

"Hello, in there!" shouted a high, falsetto voice. "If you give me the boy, you'll be spared. If not, I'll just get him anyway."

Evan shouted, "Go to hell! You're the one who oughta be scared! Give yourself up before I make you look like a poor excuse for Swiss cheese!"

Shadow said, "You should've said that you would hunt him down, rip his head off while he was still alive, and then laugh while his dead body twitched and blood spurted from his neck. That's much scarier than Swiss cheese."

Corey's eyes rounded as he stared at Shadow. "I'll say."

Evan said, "Now is not the time to criticize my intimidation tactics."

The eerie voice said, "You have two choices; send out the boy or die."

"Can any of you tell where he's standing?" Evan whispered.

"To my right," Win said.

"Shadow, douse that fire and put those eyes of yours to use. Look out the window and see what you can see," Evan said.

Shadow saw the bucket of water near the table and quietly pulled it over to him. Then he crawled over to the fireplace and slowly poured water over the flames until they were out. Removing his glasses, he drew his gun, and moved over to the window.

Evan shouted, "You're gonna have to come in here to get him, because I'm not giving him to you!"

A hair-raising, maniacal laugh followed his statement. "Oh, what fun we're having, Sheriff!"

Shadow saw a figure moving a little closer to the shack. Quickly, he fired through the glass. The figure jerked and Shadow ran to the door, throwing it open, and firing again. The person went down and Shadow ran from the cabin followed by Evan, who covered Shadow while the deputy rolled the fallen man over. He wore a silver masquerade mask, which Shadow removed.

"Ian?" Shadow queried, checking for a pulse.

Evan looked down sharply. "Ian Tomkins? The postmaster?"

"The very same," Shadow said, stunned. "I never would have believed he had that kind of darkness him."

"Is he dead?" Evan asked.

"Yes. I'm sorry," Shadow said. "He could have given us more information."

Evan swore. "It's ok, Shadow. We were pinned down and didn't know how many lunatics were out here. You did just fine."

Shadow was perplexed about feeling badly for killing someone who'd been intent on doing the same thing to them. He was further confused by how much Ian's duplicity hurt. Ian had always been friendly, helpful, and law abiding. None of them had suspected that he'd been behind such heinous acts.

He shook his head. "People think I'm insane, but I've never pretended to be anything other than what I am. Andi urged me to let in more light, but it's just too dark at the bottom, and I've never said otherwise. I thought Ian was a good man. I don't understand, Evan. Can you explain it to me?"

The moonlight illuminated the bewilderment in Shadow's eyes, and Evan felt badly for him. "Being betrayed is hell, Shadow, and it's hard to know who's capable of it. Ask Marvin more about it, because he's good at deception and disloyalty. I've never betrayed anyone in my life, so I don't have that answer. At one time, I thought Marvin was a good man, too."

Shadow frowned. "But you don't now?"

Evan put his gun away. "Frankly, Shadow, I don't know what the hell Marvin is. Let's get Ian to the undertakers, and Win can take Skyhawk home."

Shadow nodded, but his mind wouldn't let the situation alone as they went about their job.

Chapter Thirteen

Zeb sat out on the porch at the Indian school, watching some of the kids play baseball late one cold afternoon. Skyhawk sat close by, fuming because he couldn't participate. Zeb understood what that was like since he'd been in the same boat with his concussion. He was happy to now be on the way to a full recovery, but Skyhawk wasn't as lucky. He was going to be laid up for a while because of his damaged Achilles tendon.

The night Skyhawk had gotten hurt, he and Cade had stayed at the school to keep Dog Star calm, since the boy had kept trying to go find his friend. Dog Star had actually attacked Zeb because he wouldn't let him leave. Dog Star was a strong boy and his intense emotions had given him added strength, so it had been a good thing that Cade had been there to physically restrain him.

Normally, Zeb wouldn't have had difficulty defending himself against a boy, but he still hadn't been up to par and sudden movement still caused him to become dizzy sometimes. If Cade hadn't stepped in, Zeb wasn't sure that he'd have been able to keep Dog Star home. Once he'd calmed down, Dog Star had apologized to both men. Zeb had told him that they understood why he was so worried, but that that kind of behavior wouldn't be tolerated. Zeb hadn't tacked on any more time to Dog Star's punishment, figuring that he'd already been through enough.

However, Lance had taken away some of the privileges that both boys had earned back. Neither boy had put up much of a fuss, which had been surprising. Zeb figured it was probably because some sense had been scared into them and that they knew they'd deserved it.

Zeb's attention was pulled back to the present when Gray Dove came running out of the house. "*Ného'e*! Can I go—"

"He is not your father, you stupid girl!" Skyhawk shouted in Cheyenne. "He is a military captain who has been stuck here by his chiefs! He is no one's father, especially not an Indian's! Get that through your thick skull!"

Zeb had gotten out of his chair by this point. "Do not ever speak to her like that again! She's little and doesn't understand." He understood more Cheyenne than people realized. Gray Dove took a couple of his fingers in her hand and tugged. Looking down at her, Zeb saw tears in her eyes.

"*Ného'e*?"

Zeb knelt on one knee by her and thought, *this is my chance to correct her*. However, when he opened his mouth to respond, the words lodged in his throat. He *could've* corrected her, but he didn't *want* to correct her. He ran a hand over her hair, and then took her little chin in his hand.

Smiling, he said, "Yes, *Ného'e*."

She threw her arms around his neck and he hugged her. He laughed and stood up with her in his arms. "Yes, I'm *Ného'e*."

A feeling like permanent sunshine blossomed in his heart. All the time that he'd been trying to figure out how to break it gently to Gray Dove that he wasn't her father, she'd been winning his heart little by little until it had begun feeling wrong for him to attempt to dissuade her from her belief. Zeb felt the *rightness* of agreeing with her and he knew he'd never regret it.

Skyhawk was dumbfounded by what he'd just witnessed, and he almost shook his head to clear it, certain that he was hallucinating. Zeb had just proclaimed himself Gray Dove's father. The idea filled him with … anger? No. *Jealousy*.

Skyhawk shied away from admitting any such thing to himself. He suddenly missed his father intensely and tears stung his eyes. Getting up, he grabbed his crutches, made his way inside, and hopped upstairs to the refuge of his room where he could vent his emotions.

The next morning, Edna was surprised when Zeb joined her in the parlor again.

"Do you have a few moments?" he asked, sitting down.

She cut off a piece of thread from a spool and nodded before threading it through a needle. "Certainly."

He gave a short laugh. "This is such a strange situation and yet I'm happy."

Edna smiled. "You're talking about Gray Dove, aren't you?"

"Yes, I am," he said. "I never had a fighting chance, did I?"

"No, you didn't. That's how it is with kids, though. They're little miracles and bring even more miracles into our lives that we weren't expecting," Edna said.

Zeb said, "I guess they are, at that. I certainly never expected her to come into my life, especially since I'm not married."

"You sound like Thad," Edna said.

"I suppose so, since I'm going to take a page from his book."

Edna laughed. "You look like you just sucked on a lemon."

Zeb ignored her remark. "I'd be grateful if you would write a mail-order bride advertisement for me."

Edna lowered the skirt she'd been repairing for Dewdrop to her lap. "What about Sofia?"

"You and I both know that Travis has won her. I saw her in town today and bowed out graciously. I've been too preoccupied lately with recovering from a knock to the noggin, helping with Skyhawk's recovery, and becoming a father, to have the proper time to woo a woman," he said. "Honestly, I think Travis is a better fit for her. I have no idea who's a good fit for me, so I guess I'll settle for a good fit for Gray Dove."

Edna approved. "Many men and women have done the same thing and there's nothing wrong with it. After Evan's family died, Reb and I had no hesitation about finishing raising him, and I have a feeling that you won't regret doing the same for Gray Dove."

"I agree."

"Do you have any requirements?" Edna pulled a notepad from her sewing bag that she used for writing down measurements.

"I don't know. Not young, but not old." He scratched his jaw. "I really don't know."

Edna hid her amusement over his confusion. "What was it that attracted you to Sofia?"

"Well, she's kind, intelligent and has a good sense of humor. And she's beautiful and honest," Zeb said.

"Now we're getting somewhere," Edna said. "I'm assuming that you'd like to have more children."

"Yes, I would," Zeb said. "So, she should be of childbearing age, but no one under twenty-five."

They worked for fifteen minutes to finalize the ad. As they finished, Zeb felt a sense of accomplishment, and he smiled as he went about his business that day.

Skyhawk wasn't the only who was upset about Zeb's impending formal adoption of Gray Dove. He'd started the paperwork right away. Lark wasn't pleased at all and she intended to let him know how she felt when she knocked on the door of his quarters a few nights later.

He opened it and she had to steel herself against how handsome he looked in his undershirt and uniform trousers.

"Hello, Mrs. Emerson," he said.

"I need to speak with you."

"All right. Come in," he said. "Actually, perhaps you can help me with something. I'm planning on having a couple of rooms added on to my quarters so that Gray Dove has her own room and I don't know the first thing about decorating a little girl's room."

Dark fire flashed in Lark's eyes. "That's what I want to talk to you about! You can't adopt her. It's not right."

"Well, to be fair, she adopted me first," he said. "Why isn't it right? Because I'm white?"

"Yes!"

He crossed his arms over his broad chest and gave her a hard look. "Explain that racist comment."

"You are white and you have no idea what these children have been through! Imagine being literally pulled out of your family's home, dragged kicking and screaming from your parents' arms, and shipped to some faraway place where no one speaks your language or lets you speak it either!

"And now imagine that you finally get to a place of acceptance, where you've made some sort of peace with being an orphan and being forced to learn a whole new way of life. Then one of your friends is suddenly adopted by one of the school officials, but you're not," Lark said.

"You can't because you've never had anything like that happen to you because you're white. It's not fair to all of the other children and it's not right that you're looking for some white woman to be the mother of a Cheyenne child!"

Zeb's expression darkened. "You're right. I haven't experienced any of that, Lark, but I'm not sure what you expect me to do about the other children. I'm not trying to slight any of them, but none of them except Gray Dove has ever looked at me as anything other than a target at which to aim their hatred of the army."

She bristled. "Until recently, you didn't act like anything other than an army officer! Maybe if you had, more people would have seen you as a human being instead of some wooden soldier!" Lark shot back.

Zeb's ire rose higher. "Everyone's opinions were already formed when I got here. None of this is any of your business. Not my adoption of Gray Dove and certainly not my finding a wife! I would appreciate it if you'd keep your nose out of it. If a problem arises regarding the other children, I'll deal with it, but I don't need your interference. Besides, Leah Quinn loves Otto as much as if he'd been born to her and he's half-Cheyenne."

"Yes, but Lucky lived with the Cheyenne and understands them."

"Apparently you weren't listening to me very closely the night I was telling stories," Zeb said. "I have much more respect and admiration for the Indians than you give me credit for. I *have* spent time with your people. Now, if you're done with this offensive outburst of yours, I'll thank you to leave my quarters."

Lark wasn't done. "You might understand, but unless you're specifically going to ask women if they're willing to take on an Indian child, your search will end in disaster for Gray Dove. But I have a solution."

"This is ridiculous, but go ahead. What's your idea?"

Lark's chin rose as she gathered her courage. "You should marry me."

Zeb's expression slowly changed from a scowl to disbelief and then amusement. His chuckle quickly became a full belly laugh. Lark stood with her arms akimbo, her bearing proud while she waited for him to sober.

Finally Zeb wiped away his tears of mirth and calmed down. Lark arched an eyebrow at him and he said, "Good God, you can't be serious, woman."

"I'm dead serious. I can be the kind of mother Gray Dove needs. Much better than some other woman who will only end up hating her," Lark said.

"I see." Zeb walked very close to her. "Have you read my advertisement?"

"Yes." His manly scent stirred a part of her that had long lain dormant. "I read it."

"Then you know that I'd like to have more children." He put his fingers underneath her chin, tilting it up.

Her skin tingled where he touched her. "Yes."

"Then you know what I'd expect of you."

"Yes."

"And you're willing?" he asked, intending to call her bluff. "Because I expect any woman I marry to be *very* willing. Would you be *very* willing?"

The timber of his deep voice and his close proximity wrought havoc on her senses. "Yes."

He smiled a little. "You say that now, but what happens on our wedding night?"

She swallowed. "What always happens on wedding nights."

Zeb tested her further by lowering his lips almost to hers. "Do you think you might enjoy it?"

Desire unfurled inside him, which surprised Zeb given their contentious relationship, and he could very well imagine himself enjoying it.

"Yes," she said.

He admired her courage in holding out this long, but he was determined to force her hand. "Perhaps we should try it and find out."

Lark couldn't take it anymore and firmly pressed her lips to his. Electricity arched between them. Zeb put a strong arm around her waist and cupped the back of Lark's head, holding her captive while he let his sensual side loose.

Neither was gentle as the heat between them intensified. Lark's hands glided over his hard, muscular chest before fisting in his shirt. His kisses were fierce and he held her tightly against him, bringing out the feminine animal in her. When he began unbuttoning her shirtwaist, Lark broke the kiss.

"I hate you," she said, her eyes bright with desire.

His expression held passion even as he scowled. "I have no fondness for you, either."

He continued unbuttoning her blouse and she didn't stop him as he pulled it from her skirt. Pushing her blouse from her shoulders, he bent and kissed her neck, making her shiver. That motion brought Lark back to reason and she drew back from him.

"No, we shouldn't do this," she said. "We hate each other."

Zeb ran his hand up into her hair. "But if we get married, we *will* do this, even if we hate each other. We obviously have physical chemistry. Would you deny a husband his rights?"

"What you say is true, but once we are married ..." she faltered because she couldn't refute him.

What would the difference be once they had a piece of paper between them? How would that make things any better? His large hands moved down her neck, his fingers skimming along her skin. She closed her eyes against the delightful sensations he created within her.

Zeb watched her eyelids drift downward, her dark lashes brushing against her cheeks. He hadn't expected to want her so fiercely, but she brought out a powerful reaction in him. When he ran his hands slowly back up to cup her face, he stroked his thumbs over her high, delicate cheeks.

Her lips parted and he longed to kiss her. Zeb had the skill and knowledge to seduce her, but his conscience wouldn't let him. So, even though his body cried out for fulfillment, he pulled her blouse closed and began buttoning it.

Lark opened her eyes, her brow furrowed. "I don't understand."

He met her gaze. "I've never taken a woman against her will and I won't do so now."

"You're not. I want to."

Zeb pursed his lips and shook his head. "No, you don't, Lark. Not really. Mentally it would be against your will. I've never been with a woman who didn't mentally and physically want me. I'm not speaking about love. I'm talking about being with someone because you'll enjoy yourself in all ways. You're willing to submit to prove a point, but not because you truly want me." He finished buttoning her blouse. "And that, my dear, is why we won't be getting married."

Lark's cheeks burned with embarrassment and anger, but she remained silent as she straightened her blouse and tucked it back into her skirt. Then she walked out the door without looking at him or speaking. Zeb stared at the door for several moments after she'd closed it behind her.

Then he heaved a sigh and went to get ready for bed. A little while later, as he lay in bed alone, he knew that he was in for a restless night.

Chapter Fourteen

"There you are."

Shadow looked up at his wife as she came out onto the porch. He sat in one of the rocking chairs. The moonlight fell softly on her beautiful face and he smiled at her. "Here I am."

Bree carefully settled herself on his lap and he ran a hand over her softly rounded stomach. Thinking about their baby, who was due in July, his smile broadened.

"So, my handsome husband, what's keeping you awake tonight? You haven't been sleeping well lately. Is it your body clock?"

Although Shadow had mostly adjusted to sleeping during the night and being awake during the day, there were times when his body still got confused.

"No, it's not my body clock. I'm confused about some things and I can't seem to find an answer," Shadow said.

"What's bothering you?"

"Do you think Marvin is a good man?"

Her eyebrows rose. "Yes, I do."

"Even though he's betrayed people?"

"Yes. Does this have anything to do with those murders and Ian?" Bree asked. "You haven't been the same since his capture."

"You mean since I killed him," Shadow said. "You're right. It does. I've never regretted murdering any of the people I've killed in the past, but I still feel badly about killing him. How is that possible when he killed six women, kidnapped Molly, and hurt several people with those traps? Why do I feel remorse over ridding the world of someone like that?"

Bree put her arms around his neck and kissed his cheek. "Because you were friendly with him, and you feel betrayed and hurt. Killing someone you cared about must be difficult. You knew it was necessary, but you can't help feeling badly because you liked him."

"That's what I mean. Marvin has never gone on a mad rampage and killed innocent women, but he's deceived and betrayed many people over the years. And I helped him," Shadow said. "What does that make me?"

Bree said, "Marvin was protecting you. How better to drive people away than betraying and hurting them so they didn't discover you? Before he found out about you, he wasn't like that. He did those things because he loved you so much, not because he's a bad person."

"I'm responsible for him turning into a deceitful, hateful, man who betrayed people at the drop of a hat."

Bree said, "No, you're not. Marvin chose to do those things. You didn't force him to do anything."

"But if he'd never known about me, then he wouldn't have had to do any of it," Shadow said. "I should have just d—"

Bree cut him off by roughly grabbing his face and making him look at her. "Don't you dare say that! Don't ever say it or even think it! Where would I be without you? Who would I have found to love me the way you do? Who would have protected me the way you did? Who would have shown me such kindness?" Her grip loosened and she caressed his cheek. "You're the man I was meant to fall in love with." She put her hand over his where it rested on her belly. "And you were meant to be the father of my children. Is there anything you wouldn't do to protect me or our kids?"

His reply was immediate. "No. Nothing."

"Why?"

"Because I love you more than I love myself."

Bree smiled, and Shadow was struck by her beauty once again. "And that's what Marvin did. Would you want me or the children to feel guilty about anything you might do on our behalf?"

"Of course not."

"Then you shouldn't feel guilty over anything Marvin did. If Marvin was a truly evil person, would Ronni have fallen in love with him and entrusted him with Eva? Would he have been so kind to me and trusted me?"

"I see what you're saying, I truly do."

Bree said, "But you're still confused."

"Yes. I don't know when it's all right to betray the people you supposedly care about and when it's not," Shadow said. "I would never betray anyone in our family. And I would never betray my friends. I would never pretend to be someone's friend, either. If I don't like someone, I don't like them, and I wouldn't pretend otherwise."

"What if it was to protect me? Would you pretend to be someone's friend if it protected me somehow?"

"Yes." Her meaning dawned on her. "So you're saying the reason sometimes justifies the means?"

"Sometimes," Bree said. "Now I'm getting confused, but not about your brother. He's a good man. Maybe's he's done some things in the past that were considered wrong, but haven't we all?"

Shadow grinned. "Yes, and many of those things I enjoyed." Then he frowned.

Bree said, "You're overthinking all of this. Both of you are good men and that's all there is to it. You have to let all of this other stuff go before it drives you crazy. It's not black and white. There are a lot of gray areas in life, Shadow. Come to bed, honey."

He sighed. "You're right. I'm not doing myself any favors, am I?"

She shook her head and then trailed a hand down his chest. "But I might be persuaded to do some for you."

He laughed at her naughty statement. "Really? Such as?"

She told him, and he stood up with her in his arms. "Those are very nice favors indeed. I'll be happy to reciprocate."

When they reached the top of the stairs, they found Lucas standing in their room. Shadow put Bree down.

"What's the matter, Lucas?" Shadow asked.

Lucas' gaze lowered. "I peed the bed. Sorry."

"Oh, is that all?" Shadow said. "That's nothing to worry about."

"But I a big boy an' big boys aren't s'posed to pee the bed," Lucas said.

"Sometimes you can't help it," Shadow replied. "I've done it. Almost everyone has at least once."

"You did?" Lucas gave him a disbelieving look.

"Yes, I did. There's nothing to feel badly about," Shadow said. "Now, let's get you cleaned up and back to bed."

"Will you sing the monster song?" Lucas gave him a hopeful look.

Bree hid a smile because Shadow never refused when the kids asked him to do this. Of course, there was very little he refused them.

Shadow crouched down. "Is that what happened? Did you get scared?" Lucas nodded.

"That's ok. There's nothing to be afraid of, but I'll sing the monster song just in case, ok?"

"Ok. Are you mad, Mommy?" Lucas asked.

Bree cupped his face and kissed his cheek. "No, sweetie. I'm not mad at all. You go with Daddy and I'll change your bed. Everything is all right."

Lucas gave her a small smile. "Ok."

Shadow took Lucas to the bathroom and got him cleaned up while Bree changed Lucas' bed. She'd just turned it down when Shadow and Lucas came into the room that he shared with Rory, his twin sister. Lucas was wide-awake now. He climbed up on his bed and jumped up and down.

Shadow said, "Not now, little man. It's time for you to go back to sleep. Lie down so I can sing your song."

Rory was a sound sleeper and never heard Lucas' jumping, but when Shadow started singing softly, her eyes popped open. She slid out of her bed and trotted over to them on tiptoe. Rarely did her heels touch the ground. There was nothing wrong with her ankles or feet, it was just how she liked to walk.

She clambered into bed with Lucas and got under the covers with him. "Do it again, Daddy," she said.

"Yeah, Daddy. Again?"

"Only if you sing with me," Shadow said.

They nodded enthusiastically. Shadow loved hearing their sweet little voices. As he sang with them, he wished that he'd have had someone to protect him from his monster of a father. As the song concluded and he and Bree finished tucking the twins in, he had a sudden epiphany.

He *had* had someone; Marvin. Albeit later in his young life, Marvin had come along and had literally slain the monster. Suddenly his perspective of Marvin righted again and he felt a rush of gratitude for all that Marvin had done for him.

"I'll be right back," he told Bree as they were returning to their room.

"Marvy!"

The urgent whisper from close by jerked Marvin awake. He jerked again when he saw Shadow's face near his.

"What are you doing?" Marvin whispered back. "Is something wrong?" Shadow never came in their room unannounced and vice versa.

Shadow smiled. "No. Everything is fine. I just had to thank you for everything you did for me back then. You're a good man and a great brother."

"Thank you, but couldn't this have waited until morning?" Marvin asked, perplexed. Shadow's bashful expression reminded him of when they'd been teenagers and he'd had trouble expressing himself about something.

"No. I just needed you to know that. Goodnight."

Shadow patted Marvin's shoulder and left their room, leaving Marvin to ponder what had prompted Shadow's odd visit.

Chapter Fifteen

Ever since their passionate encounter three nights ago, Zeb had a hard time keeping his eyes off Lark whenever they were around each other. He'd always thought her a beautiful woman, but her attitude towards him had always turned him off. She'd made her feelings about him known the other night, and he'd returned them.

So, why did he suddenly desire her, he wondered as he sat at breakfast? He conversed with everyone present except her, but he was aware of everything she did. The memory of that night tormented him. The way her hands had bunched in his shirt, pulling him closer, the softness of her lips, and the smoothness of her skin; all of those things were embedded in his mind and he wanted more—much more.

"Zeb."

Edna's voice interrupted his musings.

"Yes?"

"Have you gotten any letters?" Edna asked.

Lark's ears perked up, but she kept her eyes on her plate.

Zeb said, "Yes. Several, in fact. There are a couple of good candidates, too."

"That's good," Edna said.

He nodded and finished his coffee. "Thank you again for your help."

"Think nothing of it," Edna said.

"Well, I must be off. Have a good day everyone." He rose and then kissed Gray Dove's cheek. "Be good for Mrs. Emerson."

"I will, *Ného'e*," she said, smiling.

Edna saw Lark's brief, disapproving frown and wondered what the teacher was displeased about. Then she caught a flash of anger in Skyhawk's eyes and her curiosity grew. It stayed with her as she helped Ellie and Lark finish up breakfast with the kids and get them into the schoolroom to begin their day.

Lark didn't understand why she had a driving need to dissuade Zeb from marrying some other woman, but she knew it wasn't because she cared for him. Just the opposite. The only redeeming quality she found in him was his devotion to Gray Dove. It showed her that he had compassion and decency, but he'd made it clear that his compassion didn't extend to her.

However, a niggling voice in her mind said, *that's not quite true. He did have enough respect for you to stop things the other night.* She was still angry about it, though. Mainly, because she couldn't get his kisses out of her mind. There was no denying her strong physical reaction to him, and she would have slept with him that night if his morals hadn't intruded.

Her pride had made her stand up to him. She'd been trying to show him that she wasn't afraid of him or what marriage to him would entail. She hadn't counted on the sensual web he'd woven around her. Who'd known that sort of passion lurked beneath his stiff exterior? The problem was that he'd begun showing a more human side of his personality and she liked it. How could she both like and hate the man?

She didn't know, but what she *did* know was that she wasn't going to let him marry some woman who didn't understand her charges. It wasn't only Gray Dove that she worried about; she didn't want some strange, white woman coming there who would be nasty to any of them. Lark knew that there were very good white people, like the ones she worked with, but she just couldn't get the idea out of her mind that any woman Zeb married would treat the children badly.

I have to do something! An idea came to her, but did she have the courage to go through with it? For the sake of the children she hoped so.

───────◦

Zeb finished his last patrol that evening before Cade relieved him, but he wasn't tired. He didn't feel like going into town, though. After he checked on Gray Dove, who was sound asleep in her bed in the room she shared with Dewdrop, Zeb went to his quarters and poured himself a glass of brandy. Suddenly his door opened, and Lark entered his parlor. She shut and locked the door before leaning back against it.

Zeb lowered his glass, which he'd paused halfway to his mouth when she'd come in. "To what do I the pleasure of your unexpected and unwanted visit?" he asked.

Lark smiled and walked over to him, lifting the glass out of his hand. She took a healthy swallow and somehow downed the fiery beverage without making a face. Zeb's shocked expression amused her, and she chuckled.

"I'm here to finish what we started the other night," she said, giving him a coy look.

Zeb took the drink back from her and sat it down. "I'm not sure what you're playing at, but—what are you doing?"

Lark undid the sash of her green, silk robe while gazing into his dark eyes. "Don't think I haven't noticed the way you've been looking at me," she said. "I know you want me." *I hope.*

Zeb's jaw clenched. *So much for hiding your feelings, you idiot,* he chided himself.

She opened her robe, revealing a silky shift underneath. He couldn't take his eyes off her as she pulled the robe down her arms and let it drop to the floor. In fascination, he watched her pretty hand move gracefully up his bare arm, her touch awakening the hunger for her that hadn't been far from the surface over the past few days.

"I haven't been able to stop thinking about it and I can see that you haven't, either," she said, emboldened by the desire in his eyes.

There was no sense denying it. "That's true, but why would tonight be any different than then?"

Lark said, "You're a very deceiving person."

"What? No, I'm not," Zeb said.

She smiled. "You don't mean to be. There's much more to you than you let on, including your passionate side."

His nostrils flared a little as she let her hand drift down over his chest and she felt satisfaction in knowing that he desired her.

"I wasn't expecting that," she said. "Like you said, we have chemistry and I'd like to see just how much chemistry we have."

Her arms encircled his waist, and she pressed her body against his firm torso. Her lush curves resting against him made his blood race through his veins. Lowering his head, Zeb brushed his mouth over hers.

"Don't tease me, Lark. If we start this, we're not stopping. Decide now," he said, meeting her midnight gaze.

The feather-light contact with his lips made her stomach flutter with desire. "I wouldn't have come here if I didn't want you."

He claimed her lips with searing intensity and Lark tightened her hold on his body, sliding her hands over his powerful back muscles. Zeb thrust his fingers through her thick, silky mane of black hair. His heart throbbed with excitement as their kissing quickly reached a frenzied intensity.

Constantly kissing Lark, Zeb maneuvered her into his bedroom. He broke away from her a little, as he hooked a finger under the right strap of her shift. "Last chance to change your mind," he said, in a passion-rough voice.

She smiled and said, "I have not changed it."

He pulled the strap aside and kissed her shoulder. Lark couldn't deny that he excited her. It had been so long since she'd felt the touch of a man, and Zeb was virile and handsome. Despite her negative feelings for him, she was attracted to him. His hands bunched in the shift, and he pulled it up over her head.

Zeb inhaled sharply as he surveyed her bronze beauty and his desire reached a new high. He kissed her hard while she undid his belt and trousers. They slid to the floor and she backed away from him, a wanton smile on her lips. She crooked a finger at him, and he readily complied, picking her up and following her down onto the bed.

What followed was one of the most sensual, explosive lovemaking experiences of their lives. There were no words of love, but expressions of appreciation and pleasure were exchanged, and neither of them was left unchanged by what they shared.

As they lay entwined, Lark traced lazy circles on his chest. "I hate you," she said.

"I hate you, too," he said, smiling.

Rising up, she looked into his eyes before giving him a slow, thorough kiss. "I think we should hate each other some more."

"I agree," he said, embracing her.

Their lovemaking this time was languorous and held a deeper meaning. Zeb made Lark feel beautiful and wanted. He was gentle, generous and exciting; she could think of nothing but him as they passed the night in each other's arms.

Zeb was just as affected as Lark. Never would he have thought that she was capable of such passion and as their ardor finally abated, he realized that this would not be the last time they'd be together. No, he knew that his craving for her had just begun. As he held her, he wondered if they could make a go of marriage. Was he willing to risk it? Wouldn't it be a risk no matter whom he married?

Looking at his clock, he saw that it was close to morning. Gently, he shook Lark.

"It's almost time to be up."

She opened her eyes and looked at him. "All right."

As they stared into each other's eyes, something passed between them. Zeb sighed and said, "You're a very wicked woman, Singing Lark."

Her beautiful smile flashed. "I am?"

"Yes." He tugged her hair a little. "Don't think I don't know what you're up to. You've caught me in your web, little spider, but you're just as caught in mine."

Her expression sobered a little. "Yes. I admit it."

He asked, "Are you sure you want to marry me?"

"Yes. I'm sure."

"Then I suppose we should begin making arrangements forthwith," he said.

"It doesn't have to be anything fancy," Lark said. "We will talk about this later. I better go."

She slid over him to the edge of the bed and he groaned, making her laugh. He watched her get dressed, and he wanted her all over again. *I am indeed caught in her web, but I don't want to escape.* She kissed him briefly before leaving and he allowed himself a half-hour catnap.

Then he rose and dressed before going to get Dog Star up for his training. Skyhawk still wasn't able to participate, but Dog Star had decided to continue even though Zeb had said his punishment was over. He jogged up the stairs to wake Dog Star with an extra little spring in his step and a smile on his face.

Secretary of War, Preston Landry, sat behind his desk in his office, reading a letter from Captain Rawlins. He laughed intermittently as he reread it.

> *Dear Piece of Crap,*
>
> *Despite the fact that you stuck me in what I had originally viewed as a detestable post, I have actually found happiness here. I'm sure that wasn't what you had intended and it gives me even more pleasure that your efforts to punish me have been thwarted. Instead of being miserable, as you had hoped I'd be, I've found a new purpose for my life; that of a father.*
>
> *I'm also marrying Mrs. Emerson, which I'm sure will also surprise and amuse you. We're adopting one of the*

children here, Gray Dove. I'm not going to go into all the details about how all of this happened. Consider this your invitation to attend the ceremony, small as it will be.

We've scheduled it for January, 7th, so it doesn't interfere with the holidays. It would be nice if you could attend, but if you can't, I won't cry over your absence.

Sarcastically,

Captain Rawlins

Preston put the letter in his desk and called Gunther into his office.
"Yes, sir?" Gunther asked.

"Please clear my schedule for the week of January 7th. I need to take a trip on urgent business that week. I don't care what's on it. Clear it," Preston said.

Gunther hated it when Preston did this because he was the one who always took flak from the people with whom Preston cancelled appointments. But, it was his duty, so he said, "Yes, sir. I'll work on it right away."

"Thank you. That'll be all," Preston said.

Gunther left and Preston sat back in his chair, thinking how nice it would be to see how the Indian school was doing and visit with some of the people with whom he'd become friends in Echo. Then he rose and put on his coat, ready to go to his next meeting. However, he still chuckled to himself over Zeb's letter off and on.

Chapter Sixteen

"Ného'e, is Santa gonna bring us presents?" Gray Dove asked Zeb as he tucked her in one night in the middle of December.

He sat on the edge of her bed. "Of course, he is. Did you think he wouldn't?"

She hugged her teddy bear a little closer. "He didn't last year."

Zeb frowned. "He didn't?"

"No."

Zeb hid his anger. "Well, he'll bring everyone presents this year."

Gray Dove's eyes lit up. "What will he bring?"

"I don't know. We'll all have to wait until Christmas morning," Zeb said.

Dewdrop sat up in bed. "He'll bring them for all of us?"

Zeb smiled at her. She might have a sweet-sounding name, but she was feisty and often got into mischief. "That's right. Everyone will get presents from Santa."

Dewdrop got out of bed and climbed onto his lap. "Are you Santa?"

"Me? No, I'm not. I don't have a sleigh or reindeer, and I certainly don't have the sort of magic it takes to fly all over the world in one night," Zeb said.

"I wish I could fly," Dewdrop said.

Gray Dove giggled. "Where would you fly?"

Dewdrop said, "Australia."

Zeb laughed. "That's far away. You might get tired."

Her brow furrowed. "Yeah. I'll fly to Alaska to see an igloo."

"That might be better for a first trip," Zeb agreed. "Now, it's time to go to sleep, girls. Back into bed you go, Dewdrop."

She put her arms around his neck and kissed him. "Ok. Goodnight, *Ného'e.*"

Oh, no. Zeb hugged her briefly, but said, "Dewdrop, I'm not your *ného'e.*"

Gray Dove said, "Yes, you are. She's my sister, so if you're my daddy, you have to be hers."

Zeb's eyes widened. "Dewdrop is your blood sister or just your friend?"

"My real sister," Gray Dove said. "Our old father was Walks Soft and our mother was Pale Bones. Jumper is our brother."

Zeb was flabbergasted. "He is? Does anyone else know this besides the three of you?"

Gray Dove shook her head. "No. He said not to tell because they'd split us up. They split up families. But you're my daddy now and you won't let that happen, will you?"

Fury swept through Zeb, but he managed to smile at her. "No, I won't let that happen."

"Thank you, *Ného'e,*" Dewdrop said. She got off his lap and climbed back into bed.

Zeb kissed both girls' foreheads, blew out their lamp and left their room. He quickly went to Lark's room and knocked. She smiled at him when she opened the door, but it faded the moment she saw his furious expression.

"What?"

He pushed her back into her room and closed the door. "Did you know?"

120

"Know what?"

"About Gray Dove, Dewdrop, and Jumper being siblings?"

Her eyes widened in fear in the face of his anger. Then she found her voice. "Jumper confided in me a few weeks ago. His sisters don't know that he did."

Zeb grabbed her arm hard enough to hurt and his jaw clenched. "That's why you didn't want me to adopt Gray Dove. Because you knew that if I did, that Dew Drop and Jumper would want me to adopt them, too. You didn't want anyone to know that they were siblings because you were afraid they'd be split up. But if you married me, I'd be forced to take them on, too. How many others here are related?"

Tears gathered in her eyes. "I don't know if there are any other siblings here. None of the others have said anything to me. Please understand why I did what I did. I love all of the children and I'm trying to give them a good future. The army breaks up families, so that the kids don't cling to their family members instead of learning how to live a new way of life. The same way they took my son from me, but I found him again."

"You have a son? Do you have more children?" he asked.

He realized that although he knew his fiancée's body quite well now, that he didn't know her at all otherwise.

"No," she said. "Just a son."

His grip on her arm tightened. "Don't lie to me. Do you have other children?"

"No! I swear. You're hurting me."

Zeb immediately released her. "You said you found him again. Where is he?"

Lark said, "I had him when I was sixteen. My husband married me when I was fifteen."

"Fifteen? That's still a child," Zeb said. "Never mind. And your husband was white?"

"No. He was raised by white missionaries, by the last name of Emerson. They were good people. They named him Christopher, but his Cheyenne name was Speaks Truth. They visited the reservations and came to live with us one winter. Chris and I fell in love and eloped the way the Cheyenne sometimes do.

"His parents were angry, but they saw that we didn't care. We had a Christian wedding and I went to live with them. It was not long until our son was born and we loved him so much. Chris was so proud of him and we were very happy. When he was five, the military came and started rounding up our children. My in-laws tried to tell the army that our son wasn't one of the reservation children, but they wouldn't listen. Chris tried to fight them, but they shot and killed him, and took our son."

The raw pain in her eyes hurt his heart and he would have embraced her, but she held up a hand. "Don't. Until that day, I didn't hate the army. I didn't like some of the things they did, but I had never been personally mistreated by them. But, after they murdered my husband and stole my son, hate grew in my heart for them."

"And that's why you hated *me*," Zeb said. "It makes sense to me now."

"Yes. I'm sorry about that. I now know that you're not like them," she said. "I vowed to find him one day. I became a teacher at an Indian school, but when I didn't find him at that one, I requested to be sent to another school. I've spent the last ten years looking for him."

"Lark, where is your son? You said you found him. We'll go get him. I can make that happen," Zeb said.

Lark raised her chin. "We do not have to go anywhere to find him. You know him as Skyhawk."

Zeb blanched and he sat down on the chair at her small desk. "Skyhawk is your son?"

Tears spilled down her cheeks. "Yes, but he doesn't know it. No one does, except you now. I couldn't risk having him taken from me again. He wasn't taken to a school right away. They saw that he'd been taken too young.

"He was given to a family on another reservation who raised him until he was ten. They'd held off the army from taking the children there for as long as they could, but finally they took them, too. That's when he was placed at Ft. Shaw and then he came here. I've been terrified that someone would find out and separate us. At least I can see him every day and be his friend.

"I was going to tell him once he was old enough to leave the school. Even if he hates me for not telling him until then, he'll know that I did it to keep him safe." She went to Zeb. "Please don't tell anyone. Please don't let them take him from me again." Dropping to her knees before him, she bowed her head. "I'm begging you not to tell."

Knowing what a proud woman she was, Zeb knew that throwing herself on his mercy was incredibly difficult for her. His heart broke for her, Skyhawk, and all of the children. She'd been right when she'd said that he had no idea what it was like being an Indian. He knew he'd be devastated now if someone took Gray Dove from him.

What strength it had taken for Lark to relentlessly search for her son, to suffer her heartache in silence! And then once she found him, she hadn't been able to tell him her identity. He'd been too little to remember her, apparently. And what of Jumper and his sisters? He couldn't imagine having to hide the fact that he was someone's sibling for fear of being separated.

"Lark, please get up. Come here." He grasped her arms and made her rise.

Getting up on her feet, she said, "I know that you won't want to marry me now, but please don't tell anyone about Skyhawk."

Zeb pulled her down onto his lap. "I'm not backing out of our engagement, Lark. You're not getting rid of me that easily. We'll tell Skyhawk together, and I'll adopt him, along with Jumper, and Dewdrop."

Lark brushed her tears away. "You can't do that. It's too much to ask."

Zeb said, "Do you think I'm that heartless? How can I take Gray Dove and not her siblings? How can I marry you and not adopt Skyhawk? He's your son and he should know that you're his mother. He deserves the truth the same way you deserve the chance to be with your son again.

"Besides, Dewdrop called me *Ného'e*, tonight. When I tried to correct her, Gray Dove informed me that they were sisters and that Jumper was their brother. When Preston comes to our wedding, I'm taking him to task about this. I'm not sure if he'll do anything about it, but at least I'll be able to voice my anger over it."

As Lark laid her head on his shoulder, her gratefulness for his consideration of her and the children changed into love. She'd been wrong to direct her hate of the army at him. Under his usually hard exterior beat the heart of a caring, loving man.

She embraced him. "I'll never be able to thank you enough. I don't know how to tell Skyhawk so that he doesn't hate me."

He held her tighter and kissed her forehead. "We'll find the words together. You're not alone."

His kindness touched a place deep inside and she let her emotions loose. Zeb held her while she cried, stoking her back and murmuring words of comfort to her.

When her tears abated, he said, "Get some sleep and we'll talk to Skyhawk and the other three in the morning."

Lark nodded. Although she wanted to be with him, she knew that she needed some time to herself to brace for the coming conversations. "You do the same."

He smiled before kissing her tenderly, and left her to prepare for bed.

Early the next morning, Skyhawk sat on his bed in disbelief after Lark and Zeb had delivered their shocking news. He remained silent as he looked back and forth at them, trying to absorb what they'd told him. Thinking about the people he'd remembered as his parents, he tried to force his memory back further, and had a vague glimpse of a white couple smiling at him. Other than that, he couldn't recall anything and he didn't remember Lark at all.

His expression belligerent, he asked, "How do I know that what you say is true? Why should I believe you?"

Lark took off the oval locket she wore and opened it. "This is a picture of you with your father and me. It was taken shortly before you were taken from us."

Skyhawk took it from her and looked at it. Although he was little in the picture, he recognized his face. He sat on his father's lap and the three of them looked so happy. Tears pricked the backs of his eyes as he handed the locket back to Lark.

"So you really are my mother?"

Lark nodded. "Please don't hate me. I never stopped looking for you. I love you so much and when I found you, I rejoiced. I didn't say anything because I didn't want you to be taken from me again. I couldn't risk that. I was going to tell you when you were old enough to leave the school. No one could separate us then."

"Why are you telling me now?" Skyhawk asked suspiciously. Happiness over finding a parent filled him, but he couldn't help being cautious.

Zeb said, "Because the risk of you being taken away has been eliminated. I won't allow it and once your mother and I are married, I'd like to adopt you, further ensuring your safety."

Skyhawk sneered at him. "I don't want your pity. I don't need it and I don't want you to adopt me."

Zeb said, "You're right; you don't need my pity, but I'd like to help you. I've come to like you, despite your smart mouth and all of the pranks you and Dog Star pull on me. You're a smart, strong young man and even if you don't want me as a fatherly figure, I'd like to be your friend. You don't have to decide that right now. Take some time to think about it. That's all I ask."

Skyhawk thought that was fair. He nodded. "I will think about it. I'd like to speak with my mother alone."

Zeb nodded understandingly. "Of course. I'll see both of you later."

When they told Jumper that they knew he was Gray Dove and Dewdrop's brother, he became terrified and begged them not to let them be separated.

"I promised our parents that I would watch over them," he said.

Zeb said, "You have nothing to worry about, Jumper. If you're willing,

Mrs. Emerson and I would like to adopt all of you once we're married. We would never all anyone to take you from us. How do you feel about that?"

His reaction was completely different from Skyhawk's. He grinned, happy tears welling in his eyes. "You'd do that for us?"

Lark smiled. "Yes. We don't want you to be split up. You're wonderful children and it would be an honor to be your parents."

Jumper impulsively hugged her. "I promise to be a good son and my sisters will be good daughters to you."

Embracing him, Lark said, "I know you will. You're a good boy and so brave for taking care of your sisters. You should be proud of yourself for doing such a good job."

"Thank you," he said.

They talked for a few more minutes and then Lark gathered the children to begin school for the day. As she taught them, she tried not to look at Skyhawk more than usual, because she didn't want him to feel pressured in any way. But, as she moved between the different age groups to help them with their work, her heart filled with hope that he would allow her and Zeb to adopt him. She also hoped that he would see that she'd done everything out of love for him and that he'd let Zeb adopt him.

Chapter Seventeen

A powerful winter storm arrived a few days before Christmas, laying down a thick, white blanket of snow. The kids were thrilled and it was hard to get them to concentrate during school because they were so anxious to play in the fluffy foot of snow. Lark finally gave up and let them out early, feeling that they deserved the extra playtime.

She changed into a pair of men's wool trousers, and her heavy, wool men's coat and warm gloves, and joined the kids. Zeb came back from patrol and saw her throwing snowballs and helping to roll big balls of snow to make snowmen. He grinned when the children started a snowball fight, and he couldn't resist joining in.

The youngsters thought this was great and ganged up on him. Lark snuck up on him and got him in the back. He turned around and fired a missile at her, hitting her on the leg before chasing her down and tackling her. He was mindful not to hurt her, but he didn't let her get away before he'd kissed her soundly.

The kids whistled and cheered while Lark blushed and scolded him for doing such a thing in front of them.

"What's the difference? We're going to be married soon. It was just a kiss," he said, grinning.

He looked her over, loving her pink cheeks and sparkling, dark eyes. Her lips were even rosier than usual from the cold weather and activity and her smile captivated him. Over the past several weeks, he'd gotten to see that Lark was a strong, brave, and passionate woman, who cared about her students more like a mother than just a teacher. She was a good woman, and he admired her tenacity in searching for Skyhawk.

His life was brighter and full of happiness with her in it, and he was glad that she'd spoken up and seduced him. Their lovemaking was exquisite, and he was a lucky man to have found a woman who was so exciting and beautiful. As he looked down at her, Zeb felt a rush of emotion for Lark that filled his heart until he thought he couldn't possibly contain it.

He stroked her coal-black hair and gazed into her eyes. "Lark, this might not be the right time to tell you, but I just can't keep it to myself. You make me so happy, and I've fallen in love with you. I'm very honored that you're going to be my wife."

Lark's stunned expression made him smile.

"You love me?"

"Yes, as impossible as it may seem, given our previous negative feelings about each other, I do. You've let me in and I like everything about you. You're a very special woman and it will be a privilege to marry you," he said.

She hugged him around the neck and said, "I love you, too. I'm sorry I ever thought you were a terrible man. I'm proud to be the woman in your heart and to be marrying you."

Although they were happy beyond words, they only gave each other a brief kiss and got up from the ground. They chased the kids around and Cade came out to play, too. They all joined forces and made a big snow fort. Once it was completed and they'd played in it for a while, the adults felt it was time for everyone to go inside to warm up and dry off.

Their cook, Marie Engle, made hot cocoa and had baked some cookies that morning. A festive atmosphere ensued and cards and other games were played until suppertime. Once the meal was over, Zeb entertained everyone for a while with more stories about his experiences in the military. Then Ellie and Lark got the kids around for bed. After Zeb said goodnight to Dewdrop and Gray Dove, Jumper met him in the hallway.

He shuffled his feet a little and gave Zeb a shy look. "I was wondering if it would be all right to call you *Ného'e*?"

Zeb smiled and took the boy by the shoulders. "I'd like that very much."

Jumper beamed at him and hugged him. Zeb returned his embrace and patted him on the back. "Everything is all right now, Jumper."

"Thank you, *Ného'e*."

Giving his back a final pat, Zeb said, "You'd better get to bed and get some sleep. We're decorating tomorrow, so it's going to be a big day."

"Ok."

"Sleep well," Zeb said.

Jumper smiled, and trotted off to his room. Zeb went down to his quarters with a heart full of gladness. When Lark came to him later on, they fell into each other's sensual web and expressed their powerful emotions with very few words between them. The two people who had once hated each other, had come a long way and found common ground. They'd discovered a whole other side to one another, and shared a new love that burned bright and true.

Zeb had never participated in a Christmas celebration that had included children, and he was a little unprepared for how rambunctious the kids became a couple of days before the holiday. It was a joyous occasion for them because the holidays at Ft. Shaw had been rather dismal, but at the Echo Indian School, preparations for a feast were being made.

All of the kids had also been given money to buy presents for others, and they were having a great time shopping, something they'd never been able to do before. The school seemed to be in constant chaos, but it was a fun time for all.

Since the children went to church, they'd learned some Christmas carols and sang them as they did chores or helped make Christmas cookies. They discovered that Dog Star had a nice singing voice along with Dewdrop and Happy Turtle. Lance had a good tenor voice, and often conned the kids into singing with him. Edna liked hearing the handsome administrator sing and praised him for his performances, which pleased Lance.

Ellie played the small piano in the parlor for them sometimes, and he persuaded Edna to dance with him when her joints were cooperating. Several times she'd caught a look of appreciation on his face while they'd danced, which made her blush, something she hadn't done since she'd been a young woman.

Zeb had noticed it and he kept teasing Edna about it.

"You should take a chance with Lance. He's a good man, and he's a little younger than you. What do you have to lose at your age?"

Her blue eyes smiled. "It's not very gentlemanly of you to point out that I'm a little long in the tooth."

He chuckled. "And it's not very lady-like of you to keep asking me and Cade to walk around shirtless, so I think we're even."

Truth be told, Edna did feel drawn to Lance. He was only a couple of years younger than her and it was obvious that he'd taken a shine to her. Edna didn't back down from any challenge, but it had been decades since she'd been courted, and she didn't know if she wanted to be courted. Maybe they could start out just being casual companions, she reasoned. They could sort of dip their toes in and see how the water felt. She decided that if Lance asked her out, she would accept, but only if he was agreeable to such an arrangement.

On Christmas Eve, they loaded up the children and went to the church service. The kids were so wound up that, before they went into church, Zeb gave them all a stern talking to about behaving during the service. His authoritative voice got through to them and they quieted down.

Andi always put on a beautiful service, but this year they had a full choir thanks to Henley twisting arms to get those whom he knew sang well to participate. They'd all worked hard and their music added a special element to the spirit of the season. As the congregation sang Silent Night, Cade nudged Zeb's arm from where he sat behind the captain. Cade smiled and motioned over at Dog Star.

Zeb looked around casually, and saw that the boy's focus was on Pauline Desmond, who cast a couple of furtive glances the young man's way. With great difficulty, Zeb was able to keep a straight face and continue singing. Zeb showed Lark, who had to cover her mouth to muffle her tiny giggle.

Skyhawk was oblivious to his best friend's preoccupation with Pauline. He was too busy thinking over the situation with his mother and the captain. Did he want her in his life as his mother? Did he really want to be adopted by an army officer? A man who represented the very people who'd taken him away from both his real and adoptive parents?

Did he want to have a last name again? Skyhawk Rawlins didn't sound too bad, he supposed. He sighed as he thought about Zeb's refusal to turn him and Dog Star in to the military for causing his concussion. Zeb had also been kind to him since his ankle had been hurt. He'd helped him around, and had kept him company when the other kids were out playing and he'd been stuck in bed. They'd played cards, and Zeb had taught him how to play checkers and chess.

Looking over at Zeb, Skyhawk thought that those were all things that fathers did with their children. The captain's gaze met Skyhawk's and Zeb smiled at him. Skyhawk smiled back briefly and then turned around towards the front again. When he did, he saw Pauline smile at Dog Star, who shyly returned it.

Skyhawk raised his hymnal to hide his own smile, but a soft snort of laughter escaped him, drawing Dog Star's attention.

"What are you laughing at?" Dog Star asked, smiling.

"You and Pauline. So, she's gonna be your wife, huh?"

Dog Star scowled at him. "Shut up. You've got your own girlfriend, so don't make fun of me."

"What? I don't have a girlfriend," Skyhawk whispered.

"Tell that to Lyla Remington. She keeps staring at you whenever they're not singing," Dog Star said, grinning.

Skyhawk looked at the choir box and sure enough, pretty Lyla was looking right at him. His eyes widened and then he dropped his gaze to his hymnal. He looked again and she smiled at him.

Skyhawk said, "I thought she liked Porter."

Dog Star leaned towards him. "I don't think Porter feels the same way since he wants to be a bounty hunter. He's not interested in settling down. I mean, not that we are, but, well, you know what I mean."

Skyhawk didn't know what to think. Maybe it wouldn't be a good idea to encourage her, but he couldn't deny that she was pretty with her light brown hair and blue eyes. For the rest of the service, he kept his eyes averted from her.

Andi concluded the service and wished everyone a Merry Christmas before coming down from the pulpit to shake hands. She heartily thanked the choir for their fine performance and moved among the parishioners with Arliss at her side. Suddenly a chill went up her back and dizziness enveloped her.

She distantly felt Arliss steady her and then pick her up. He called to her, but she only faintly heard him. Her point of view changed, and suddenly, she was looking at herself and Arliss, but it wasn't her own eyes through which she looked. She watched Arliss lay her on a pew and pat her cheeks.

A low chuckle sounded in her head and Andi screamed inside hers, trying to push him out of her mind. Then she stilled and tried to figure out who he was. His madness made it hard, so even though she could see what he saw, she couldn't get a fix on a name. Then she was back inside herself, looking up into Arliss' worried eyes.

"He's here," she whispered.

His blue eyes widened. "Who?"

"The killer. The real one. It was a trick."

Andi sat up abruptly, and began searching the crowd in the direction she thought the killer had been standing. There were quite a few people there and none of them were acting suspicious. They were looking over at her with concerned expressions, but that was to be expected.

She smiled at Arliss and said, "I'm fine. I think I just got overheated a little. It's warm in here from all of the body heat."

Arliss knew she was saying this louder for the benefit of those around them. He helped her up, but kept glancing around where she'd been looking to see if he could detect anything. Once she was steady on her feet, Arliss walked with her as she assured everyone she was fine and gave the overheated excuse for her fainting spell.

She shook hands and briefly touched people as they moved around, but nothing came to her. He must have already left, and he could be anyone. Although she was deeply disappointed, Andi finished her duties and put it out of her mind for the moment. However, she decided that once Christmas was over, she'd tell Evan about the experience. There was nothing to be done about it right then, and she didn't want to ruin anyone's holiday.

Zeb put peppermint sticks and other candy in the last of the stockings, and smiled at the sense of completion he felt. As excited as the kids were for morning to come, he might be even more so. He was looking forward to watching the youngsters rip into their gifts and exclaim over them.

Turning around, he found Cade watching him with a smile.

"What?" Zeb asked.

Cade said, "Oh, nothin'. Just thinkin' that if I'd have known it would've improved your disposition so much, I woulda conked you on the head right when I first met you. You've changed since then."

Zeb tried to give him a steely look, but he couldn't quite manage it. "I'm still your superior officer, Cade, so don't think about hitting me every time I do or say something you don't like."

Cade laughed. "I didn't plan on it."

"But you're right. I think it's because I was forced to associate with everyone on a much more human level than just a protector or an enemy, depending on who you were," Zeb said. "And it doesn't hurt that I'm marrying the woman I love, either. Or that I've acquired a passel of cute kids."

"I never thought you'd get married before I did," Cade said. "I'm happy for you, though. Lark's a good woman and those kids will give you a lot of joy."

Zeb smiled. "All of them already do."

"I'm glad to hear it. Well, I'm heading out for patrol. See ya in the morning," Cade said.

"Cade, don't stay out all night. It's cold and it's Christmas. I don't think any mischief makers are about, since it's the holiday."

Cade's blue eyes held surprise. "Are you giving me permission to knock off early?"

"Yes, I am," Zeb said, testily. "I'm not Ebenezer Scrooge for Pete's sake."

"Ok. I'm gonna take you up on that," Cade said, putting on his coat. "See you in the morning."

"Goodnight," Zeb said.

Cade left, and Zeb went to the schoolroom where Ellie and Lark were putting away a few things in a closet. Lark closed, locked it, and caught sight of Zeb. She felt the familiar jolt of attraction the sight of him always caused. Her feelings were reflected in his eyes as he watched her move about.

Ellie wished them Merry Christmas and went to go check on the children before retiring for the night. Lark blew out the lamps in the schoolroom and went to Zeb.

"All finished out there?" she asked.

"Yes. All of the candy has been distributed as per your orders, madam," he said, clicking his heels together and giving her a smart salute.

She giggled. "Very good, Captain. I'll give you a reward—tomorrow night."

Zeb sagged. "*Tomorrow* night?" he asked petulantly.

Lark was always surprised when he acted silly like that. "Yes. I don't want to take the chance that any of the children will be up and about."

"Ok." He gave her a hangdog expression and then smiled. "I agree. May I escort you to the bottom of the stairs?"

She shook her head and took his arm. He walked very erect, in an exaggerated attention pose, which made her laugh. Upon reaching the stairs, they kissed goodnight, and Lark went upstairs, wishing she was staying with Zeb. Soon, though, she would be with him every night. That thought kept a smile on her lips as she slipped into bed and blew out her lamp.

When Zeb went to his quarters, he found that a note had been slid under his door. Picking it up, he read, "Once you and Mother have married, I will sign my name as Skyhawk Rawlins."

Zeb knew that he'd been given one of the best Christmas presents he would ever receive. Skyhawk's trust was a rare gift and he would take very good care of it. He didn't delude himself into thinking that the boy would be easy to finish raising, but Zeb felt that it would be worth it to help Skyhawk be the man he sensed he could be. Knowing that he wasn't going to sleep for quite a while, Zeb poured a drink and sat down in one of his chairs in front of the fire. Staring reflectively into the flames, he pondered how much his life had changed, and he spent the remainder of the night reliving it all and thinking about the future.

Chapter Eighteen

The kids were already up when Ellie went to wake them. They'd dressed, but they hadn't gone downstairs, as per her orders. When she released them, their footsteps created thunder on the stairs as they hurried down them. Skyhawk came last, since he still had some flexibility issues, but all in all, he was happy with the way his ankle was healing.

He saw Zeb waiting in the foyer for him and stopped in front of him. Zeb said, "I got your note last night."

Skyhawk raised an eyebrow. "Oh?"

Smiling, Zeb held out a hand to him. Skyhawk returned his smile and shook Zeb's hand. Nothing more needed to be said between them. Together they went to the parlor where all the kids sat very quietly, just looking around at all of the presents. They were stymied as to what to open first.

Skyhawk said, "What are you waiting for? You can read! Find your name and open them!"

His order snapped the children out of their shock and a free-for-all began, with kids passing presents to one another when they found each other's names.

As they sat back watching all of this, Zeb said to Lark, "I see that Skyhawk has inherited your bossiness."

She smiled serenely at him. "You just lost your reward."

He frowned and then chuckled. "Earning it back could be fun."

Lark stifled a giggle. "We'll see."

"Yes, we will," was Zeb's firm reply.

The students showed all the adults the presents that "Santa" had brought for them. Soon, some of the kids began playing with their toys and games. Others, like Jumper, read their new books or looked over their new clothing. However, Skyhawk and Dog Star, hadn't been handed any presents.

The boys looked at each other in confusion, but never said anything, not wanting to appear rude or petty. Zeb didn't let it go on much longer. He went back to his quarters and brought out two big, rectangular boxes, handing one to Dog Star and one to Skyhawk. He just smiled when they gave him questioning looks.

"Open them," he said.

They did and each held up fine, leather halters, decorated with turquoise and silver accents.

"I don't understand," Dog Star said. "What are we supposed to do with these?"

Lark laughed. "You're a smart boy. What do you usually do with a halter?"

The boys looked at each other as disbelieving smiles spread over their faces. Then Dog Star raced from the room, with Skyhawk running slowly after him. They were so excited, that they forgot to put on any footwear, running over the hard-packed snow path to the barn in only their socks.

Dog Star stopped just outside the barn, waiting for Skyhawk.

"Do you really think they got us horses?" he asked.

"Only one way to find out," Skyhawk said.

"I know, but I'm afraid to hope."

"Me, too, but we can't stand here."

"Ok. Let's go."

The entered the barn, and on each of the two crossties stood a horse. Slowly, the boys approached the horses so they didn't scare them. These weren't just any horses. The Appaloosas were fine, gorgeous animals. One was a mostly black stallion with black-and-gray dappled hindquarters. The other, a mare, was a bay roan, with only a small patch of spots on its rump.

"I'll take the mare," Skyhawk said. "She's a beauty."

"They both are. Ok. I don't mind having a stallion. I'm surprised that they're not both geldings," Dog Star said.

Zeb's voice made them turn away from the horses. "They're not geldings because we thought you boys might like to try your hand at breeding some Appaloosas."

"Really?" Skyhawk asked. "I'd love that. Thank you."

Dog Star nodded. "Thank you. We'll take great care of them."

"We know you will," Cade said. "Any Indian worth their salt cares more for his horse than himself, so we know they're in good hands."

Lark asked, "What are you going to name them?"

Skyhawk said, "Well, Mother, I think I'll name mine She Who Has Lots of Babies."

The rest of the school came out to the barn, and they laughed at his joke.

Lark felt like all the wind had been knocked from her. "What did you call me?"

Skyhawk limped over to her. "I called you Mother. That's what you call your mother, you know. For a teacher, you're not very smart."

She laughed through her tears and hugged him close while everyone except Zeb wore confused expressions. Lark kissed his cheek, looked into his eyes, which were on the same level as hers now, and then hugged him again.

In Cheyenne, she said, "My son, no one will ever take you from me again. I love you so much, and my heart is filled with joy to be with you again."

Skyhawk blinked back tears. "Thank you for not giving up on me, Mother. I am sorry that I do not remember you."

"Do not worry about it. We are together again. That is all that matters," she said.

Parting, they smiled at each other, and then looked around at the others.

Dog Star frowned. "Mrs. Emerson is your mother?"

Skyhawk saw the hurt and anger in his friend's eyes. "Yes, but she could not tell me until a couple of weeks ago. You know they split up families. If anyone had known, they would have taken me from her again. I was going to tell you, but I was not ready yet. I had some things to decide."

Dog Star hid his pain behind an understanding smile, not wanting to look bad in front of everyone. "I am happy for you. It is only right for you to be with your mother." He stroked his stallion's neck, pretending to become engrossed with the animal. "Let's get your halter on you. I have no idea what to name him yet, but a name will show up," he said brightly. "One always does."

Skyhawk knew Dog Star better than anyone and he saw that Dog Star was far from happy. However, he let it go for the moment. They would talk more in private. For now, the boys put their horses' halters on and then put them in their stalls. Then they were ushered back to the house to change into dry socks and get warmed up, since they had run outside without their coats, too.

All through the holiday, the school was filled with laughter and happiness. The children were so grateful for everything they'd received, that they didn't gripe one bit as they helped cart their loot up to their rooms and put it away. Zeb had more fun than he could ever remember having at holiday time.

He spent time with all of the kids, not just the ones whom he was adopting. They each had their own unique personalities, and they made him laugh when they teased him, or each other. Lark watched him, and thought that it had been a shame that he'd never had children before.

Then she understood that the Great Spirit had been saving him for her and the four children he was adopting. If he'd already been married when he'd come to this post, they wouldn't have fallen in love with each other and they wouldn't be adopting children together.

Although her past had been painful, Lark now knew that it was the

Great Spirit's plan to bring the people together whom were meant to be. That knowledge helped ease her bitterness over losing so much time with Skyhawk. It would be foolish to waste any more time with regrets, instead of enjoying the present, and looking forward to the future.

As the special day drew to a close and she helped tuck in children and say goodnight to them, peace and contentment settled on her shoulders, and she felt a lightness in her soul that had been missing for a long time.

January 7th dawned cold and clear, but no one seemed to notice the temperature at the Indian school. There had been a change of venue for Lark and Zeb's wedding since Mother Nature had dumped more snow on them right after New Year's, making it unfeasible to haul the kids back and forth to the church for the short time they'd be there.

Instead, everyone was coming to the Indian school for the ceremony. Several people in the area had sleighs, including Jerry, and they were being used to transport wedding guests. Zeb and Lark had been both dismayed and honored to find out that there were many more people to invite than they'd first thought.

Edna had said, "You have to invite all of the town officials and everyone who has anything to do with the school, too. You don't want to slight anyone."

Zeb had said, "Meaning your nephew and his staff."

"Exactly," Edna had said with a chuckle. "But you'll want to—oh, it'll just be easier for me to make you a list."

Many hands were on deck preparing the wedding feast, and a few women had come to help dress all of the girls, so that Lark could concentrate on her own appearance. She'd been married before, so she didn't wear white. Instead she'd chosen a deep maroon, silk-and-lace dress that was appropriate for the season, and for a woman who'd been previously wed. It also went well with her coloring.

Cade had offered to walk Lark down the aisle, but Skyhawk had objected, insisting that he would give his mother away. Since his acceptance of Lark as his mother, he'd become very protective of her. Lark had reprimanded him and made him apologize to Cade, but she had still allowed Skyhawk to be the one to lead her to Zeb, touched that he wanted to do so. Lark had asked Ellie to be her maid of honor, and Zeb had chosen Cade as his best man.

Zeb was tense, pacing back and forth in his parlor as Cade looked on. He'd never seen his superior so nervous, and it was amusing.

He chuckled. "Zeb, calm down. You're not going before a general or something. You're marrying the woman you love."

Zeb speared him with a sharp glance. "Yes, I know, but I don't want to fail as a husband or a father. Just wait until it's your turn."

"Funny you should mention that," Cade said. "I was wondering if you still had those letters from women. Maybe one of them wouldn't mind stepping down from a captain to a corporal. I'd be happy to explain the situation to them."

Zeb smiled. "So you've been thinking about matrimony. Yes, I have them and you're welcome to them."

"Thanks. There's no rush for them," Cade said.

"They won't be settling for a corporal, Cade. I'm recommending you for a promotion to sergeant for all of the excellent work you do," Zeb said.

Cade stared at him for a few moments and blinked. "You are?"

"You deserve it. I've already spoken to Preston about it, and he agrees. It's not official yet, but it shouldn't be too long until it is."

Cade held out a hand and they shook. "I can't thank you enough."

"I can't thank you enough, for always helping me, even though you didn't like me very much. I hope we can be friends and not just fellow soldiers," Zeb said.

"We already are, Zeb."

"Glad to hear it."

Arliss came to get the men.

"Well, you both look good. I'm real happy for you, Zeb. Lark is a good woman and I'm really impressed that you're taking on all those kids," he said.

Zeb still didn't fully understand about Arliss' disorder and he was often uncomfortable around him. "Thanks, Arliss. I finally picked the right woman and who wouldn't fall in love with our brood?"

"Well, they're getting good parents," Arliss said. "Are you ready?"

Zeb squared his shoulders and nodded. "Yes. Ready."

"You look beautiful, Mother," Skyhawk said.

"Thank you."

"Are you nervous?"

Lark smiled. "No. Yes. A little."

Skyhawk laughed. "Well, that clears that up."

"Hush, my son." It felt so good to be able to call him that. "If you're here, it means that it's time."

He nodded. "Ready?"

"Yes, I am ready."

Chapter Nineteen

Ellie played the Wedding March as Skyhawk walked his mother down the aisle. Pride showed in his erect posture, and he was able to walk almost normally. His ankle was getting better all the time and would soon be fully healed.

Lark was surprised that Zeb wasn't wearing his dress uniform. Instead, his fine physique was encased in a perfectly tailored gray tuxedo, and he looked even more handsome, if that was possible. The gleam in his eyes told her that he found her beautiful. She couldn't believe that she was marrying the man she'd viewed as her enemy for so long, but she was ready to join her life with his.

Watching the easy, graceful way Lark walked, Zeb thought her the most gorgeous woman on the planet. Her hair had been pulled back and secured with beautiful golden hair combs. His heart beat a little faster at the appreciation he saw in her eyes. Their physical connection was powerful, but the emotional bond they'd formed was even more so. Who'd have thought that their previous contentious relationship would turn to one of love? Certainly not him, but he was grateful for the happiness they now shared.

When they arrived at the front of the schoolroom, Skyhawk gave Zeb a hard look, and then smiled as he gave Lark's hand to Zeb. Then he sat by Dog Star and glanced at him. Although they'd talked about the circumstances around the discovery that Lark was his mother, Dog Star still remained slightly aloof. Skyhawk didn't know what to do to make it better, so he just left it alone, hoping that with time Dog Star would feel better.

Zeb held Lark's hands and smiled into her eyes as Andi began the ceremony. Their vows were said with conviction and they felt drawn closer with every word they uttered. When it came time, their kiss was a symbol of their commitment, but it also represented their deep feelings for one another.

The guests applauded the newlyweds, with the children clapping and cheering noisily. They laughed and were surrounded by the kids and other well-wishers. As he shook hands, Zeb glanced at Lark's left hand often, loving the way her wedding band looked. He felt possessive and the ring was an outward symbol letting everyone know she now belonged to him.

She caught him looking at her and smiled. "What?"

"You're ravishing, but I was expecting you to wear a Cheyenne dress," he said, his eyes filled with mischief.

"And I was expecting you to wear your dress uniform," she said.

He smiled. "I guess it's a good thing neither of us wore them. We probably would have looked like we were going to war instead of getting married."

Preston overheard them. "Congratulations to you both, but I'm of the opinion that marriage is exactly like war. Hence the reason I got divorced. Of course, I know that won't happen with you."

Lark laughed, while Zeb glowered at him.

"I hardly think those are appropriate sentiments to air on this occasion," he said.

Preston made a gesture of surrender. "Pardon my faux pas. I really do wish you all the best. You have your work cut out for you, Mrs. Rawlins."

Lark's eyes widened when he used her new last name. She'd almost forgotten that her name would change. It pleased her immensely to now be

Mrs. Zebadiah Rawlins. Looking at Zeb, she saw that he was thinking the same thing, and she beamed at him. He put an arm around her and squeezed her shoulder.

She rested her hand over his for a few moments, and then they were taken out to the dining room for the reception, which spilled over into the parlor. It was an intimate, noisy affair that everyone thoroughly enjoyed.

As Preston watched Zeb and Lark, he thought how strange it was that Zeb would have this kind of wedding. He'd always pictured the captain marrying some blue blood gal in a big church and having a reception in a fancy ballroom. He found that he much preferred this reception to the more formal kind.

Zeb would've been shocked to know that he and Preston were thinking the same thing. Whenever he'd pictured his wedding and reception, he'd never seen himself wedding a Cheyenne woman, and eating his reception dinner with a little Indian girl on his lap. However, he was having the time of his life, and he wouldn't change one thing about it.

The schoolroom had been changed from a chapel into a small ballroom, and not only did Ellie play, but Henley accompanied her on his fiddle and he and Marvin sang together. Eventually, Marvin convinced Josie to sing with them.

As Zeb and Lark danced together, quite a few people remarked what an attractive couple they made and Skyhawk overheard them. He had to admit that they were right and he was happy for the newlyweds and himself. Someone tapped him on the shoulder and he looked at Dog Star.

"Come with me," Dog Star signed.

Skyhawk followed him outside. "What is it?"

Dog Star said, "It's about this whole thing with your mother. I'm not jealous of you. I'm happy for you. I really am. I was just hurt because you're like my brother, and we always tell each other everything. I've been thinking about it, and I understand why you didn't tell me this. You had a lot to think about, and there are things that people have to figure out for themselves. I'm not mad anymore."

Skyhawk said, "I'm glad. I really wasn't trying to hurt your feelings. I was caught off guard, and I didn't know which end was up. You're right, I had to think it through on my own and I told Mother first because it was only right that she knew first. In my heart, you *are* my brother, and I've always told you everything else."

Dog Star nodded. "Ok. So this is over and done. Agreed?"

"Agreed."

They grasped arms and grinned at each other, relieved that their bond was fully restored.

Zeb's internal clock told him it was time to get up, but he hadn't been asleep all that long anyway. It was the morning after their wedding, and they hadn't done much sleeping. The sun was just peeking over the horizon.

Lark's warm, luscious body lay draped halfway over him and he loved the way she felt against him.

"Lark," he whispered, shaking her a little.

"Hmm?"

"Look."

Raising her head, she saw a few rays of sun streaming through the window in their bedroom.

"The sun is coming up, but you don't have to rush off anymore. Isn't that wonderful?"

She giggled against his chest and pressed a kiss to it. "Yes, it is. It feels so strange to not have to help get the children around for school."

"Yes, and it feels strange to not be going out on patrol," Zeb said. "However, Cade is more than capable of keeping an eye on things."

"And I'm more than capable of keeping my eye on you." Lark rose up and kissed him. "From where I'm sitting, you look damn good."

Zeb laughed over her statement as she nuzzled his neck, tickling him. Then she bit him, and he growled.

"Unless you're ready for round …" He paused and then grinned. "I've lost count. Anyway, unless you're prepared for another round, I suggest you don't do that."

With a wicked smile, Lark lowered her head and bit his neck again. She squealed as he rolled her over, and took her on yet another sensual journey before they settled in for some actual sleep. It was early afternoon before they made an appearance. Ellie and Edna were teaching the children from the lesson plans that Lark had made up ahead of time. The newlyweds avoided the classroom so they didn't distract the kids from their studies.

They made some lunch, and sat talking quietly in the kitchen about whatever came to mind. The next week followed much the same pattern. They visited with everyone, but spent plenty of time alone, even going to Dickensville for a couple days, once the roads were clear enough for a buggy.

During their previous discussions, they'd decided to build a house on the school property for them and their four children. They didn't feel that it was right that Ellie still take care of their kids, and they also wanted to be able to have private time with them.

As they drove home from Dickensville, they talked more in depth about their building plans. They'd decided to build an extra room to use as a nursery in case they needed it, which they hoped they would.

Arriving home, they were greeted enthusiastically by everyone, with all of the kids trying to talk to them at once. Dog Star insisted on helping them with their luggage, which struck Zeb as strange, but he didn't refuse the offer.

Once they had taken their things to the newlyweds' quarters, he asked, "Captain, can I talk to you a minute?"

"Certainly," Zeb said.

Lark took the other kids out to the kitchen to give them privacy.

Dog Star shifted nervously on his feet. "How do you ask to see a girl?"

Zeb kept his smile small, even though he wanted to grin. "You have a young lady on your mind, hmm?"

Dog Star smiled bashfully. "Yeah. I think she likes me, too. How do I ask to see her?"

Zeb motioned for them to sit down, and he walked Dog Star through the steps for courting a woman. "However, at your age, I don't think you could call it courting. I think 'seeing' her is a good term. May I ask who the young lady is?"

"Pauline Desmond," Dog Star said.

"Ah, yes. A very pretty young lady." Zeb gave Dog Star a considering look. "This is something that normally a father does, but has anyone explained to you about the birds and the bees?"

"No," Dog Star said with a nervous laugh.

"Do you want me to? I'd be happy to, but only if you're comfortable with it," Zeb said.

Dog Star nodded. "Yeah. I'd appreciate it."

Zeb began. "Well, you see…"

A half hour later, Dog Star left Zeb, his mind working on all that had been imparted to him about what happened between men and women. He somehow felt more mature and yet scared. It was a strange combination of emotions. Needing some time alone to process the new information, he went out to the barn to see his stallion.

By then end of February, the adoption papers had come through for all four kids and the Rawlins family had settled into a nice routine. They couldn't wait until their house construction began in May, but in the meantime, they spent their days much the same way they always had, but their nights were spent together, instead of Zeb trying to find something with which to occupy his time.

He was involved in all aspects of the children and Lark's life, and it made him feel wanted and needed. However, he never shirked his duties, and always made sure the school was safe. Since he was now emotionally attached to the other people there, his job took on new meaning and he was extra careful when out on patrol, making sure to miss nothing that could possibly threaten his loved ones.

Lark fell more in love with her husband every day, and closer to their children, too. Her life, too, had more meaning. She loved watching Zeb with the kids and learned more about her husband all the time. It was a time of great joy and she thanked the Great Spirit time and again for all of the blessings that He'd given to her.

Chapter Twenty

Zeb stopped at the Express office to pick up a paper, and greeted Molly who was due to have her baby in May. She was a strong young woman and had recovered from awful experience quickly. Molly hated wearing dresses, but she didn't have much choice since her jeans no longer fit her.

"How are you feeling?" Zeb asked.

"Fat, but other than that, just fine," she replied.

He smiled. "Well, you don't look fat."

"Thanks. I think Dan has a telegram for you," Molly said.

"Oh. Thank you."

Once he'd collected it from Dan, Zeb bid the both of them goodbye, and went outside to read the missive. His eyebrows rose and a grin spread across his face as he read it. Elated, he got on his horse and rode home at a canter to spread the good news.

Lark listened to Zeb with a sinking feeling in her heart and she couldn't say anything once he was finished.

He gave her a puzzled look. "I take it that you're not happy about this news."

She wasn't sure how to answer him and she took a couple of moments to gather her thoughts. "Zeb, I can't tell you how proud of you and happy for you I am."

"But?"

"I don't want to leave here," Lark said. "I know that you're excited about this post they're offering you and you deserve it, but I love it here, and I have no idea what I would do in Washington. I doubt there are any schools that will hire an Indian. Besides, I don't have that sort of degree."

Zeb said, "I wouldn't want your skills to go to waste, Lark. With the increase in my pay, you wouldn't have to work per se. You could volunteer to help poor children with their schooling. You'd still be teaching, which I think is your calling."

"Zeb, our kids aren't going to be welcomed in the schools there, and you know it. Even if they did, Skyhawk would never adjust. The younger kids would in time, but not him," Lark said.

She was right. With Skyhawk's attitude, he'd wind up in fights left and right, and he'd be kicked out of any school he attended.

"No, Washington schools wouldn't agree with him," Zeb agreed. "But appointments like this don't come around every day, Lark. I can't just pass it up."

"I know how important this is to you, but you're a father now and parents have to put their children ahead of themselves."

"Don't be condescending, Lark. I'm well aware of that. The children will want to attend college someday, and there will be schools that will no doubt accept Indians by then. We'll need the increase in my salary to cover their expenses. And if we have a baby—"

"I don't think that's a good idea," Lark said. "I won't subject another child to the sort of racism they'll encounter in Washington."

Zeb stared at her. "You don't want a baby?"

Lark shook her head. "Not if you take this appointment. I knew that marrying you meant that I might have to move someday, but I didn't think it would happen so soon. I thought we'd at least get Skyhawk raised before it did."

"Are you using the children as leverage to stop me from taking the job?" Zeb said. "The problem is that I don't think that this is a request. Just like I didn't have a choice about coming here, I don't think I'll have a choice about this new post."

"I would never use them as pawns, Zeb," Lark said, her tone cool. "I understand that you have to do what they tell you, but I won't bring a baby into that sort of situation."

Zeb let out a sarcastic laugh. "Well, unless you don't ever intend to make love with me again, it could happen. There are no foolproof prevention methods."

"I know," She said. "Why did this have to happen? We've been so happy."

Zeb blew out a breath. "Yes, we have. There has to be a solution. Let's put our heads together and come up with one, instead of fighting. Come here."

Smiling, she got out of her chair and went to sit on his lap.

Settling her in, Zeb said, "Let's not get ahead of ourselves. I have to go to Washington to talk with them about it. Now, here's what I'm willing to do; if they're not forcing me to take the appointment, then I won't. I'll stay here until Skyhawk is grown, but if another appointment comes up after he is an adult that I like, then we'll go. Does that sound reasonable?"

She held his gaze for several moments. "I'm very sorry, Zeb. I underestimated you again. Yes, that's very reasonable—and very generous. Thank you. Now, what if they won't take no for an answer?"

"Then we give Skyhawk a choice of whether to come or stay here," Zeb said. "He can come to Washington for the summers."

Fire leapt into Lark's eyes. "No. I won't lose any more time with him. Once he's eighteen and if he wants to leave home, there's nothing I can do about it, but I'm not missing any more of his childhood than I already have."

"Be reasonable, Lark. *I* am. I'm willing to make a compromise for our family's sake, why can't you?"

She got off his lap and walked over to the window, looking out of it while she worked to stay calm. Looking at him, she said, "Leaving Skyhawk behind isn't what's best for him, but neither is taking him to Washington. If they force you to take this appointment, we'll join you in the summers until he's eighteen and then me and the others will move to Washington."

Zeb got up, his face slightly pink with anger. "So I'm supposed to leave all of you behind and go to Washington alone for three years?"

Lark crossed her arms over her chest. "You're an adult; he's not. You're better equipped to get through something like that, the same way I am. I don't want to be without you, either, but I have to put his needs ahead of my own."

Zeb said, "You're wrong. I've never been married with a family before—a family I adore, by the way. Call me soft, but I don't want to lose time with our kids, either."

Lark tried to keep a level head, but in her mind, she saw their happy future going up in flames. "If you take this appointment and we went with you, you'd be working all the time anyway. You wouldn't be home much, so what's the difference?"

"The difference would be that I could be around much more than if half the country separates us. I would be much more accessible than if you were all still here," Zeb said.

"So, we would have to wait until you were 'accessible' to us. How typical of a military man."

Zeb was stung. "Excuse me? Tell me something, my dear; what happens when Indian braves go off to war or on an extended hunting trip? How accessible are they to their family at such times? Do they have telephones or a telegraph machine with which to contact their loved ones? I think not.

"By accessible, I mean that you or the kids would be able to call me every day at lunch time if I'm in my office, or I could call home. It would be very nice for me, too, to be able to hear your voice during the day when I miss you all. My voice carries well, but you won't hear me here in Montana, no matter how loudly I yell while standing in downtown Washington!

"And here's another idea in the spirit of compromise, Lark; you could homeschool our children and then they could take state boards for their diplomas. You're perfectly qualified. Under those conditions, Skyhawk might actually like Washington. There are plenty of country homes outside the immediate city, and I could probably get Preston to help me twist some arms to get us a nice place with some land because Dewdrop loves working in the garden and Skyhawk would have a place to ride and woods to explore!

"Gray Dove loves any sort of frilly clothing and God knows there are enough boutiques in Washington to satisfy her every whim. And I haven't forgotten about Jumper. The boy is book-hungry, and they have great big libraries in Washington! But, again, I'm just being a typical military man and not putting my children's needs ahead of my own, right?"

Zeb grabbed his coat, put on his hat, and stormed out of their rooms through the door leading straight to the outside. He rammed right into Skyhawk.

"What?" he asked in a cutting tone.

Skyhawk recoiled from him. He'd never seen Zeb so angry before. "Nothing. I was just taking a walk," he lied. It was the first thing he could think of.

"Oh. All right. I'll leave you to it, then." Zeb marched to the barn, saddled a horse, and rode away.

It was with a heavy heart that Zeb boarded the train in Helena that would carry him to Washington. Saying goodbye to his family, even temporarily, was incredibly difficult. However, he didn't have a choice, so he did what he was good at; put his personal feelings on hold and got on with the job.

Taking his seat on the train, he looked out at the platform where the children stood waving at him. Skyhawk had hoisted Gray Dove onto his shoulders, and he walked close to the train, so she could put her little hand against his compartment window. Laughing, he put his hand up to hers for a few moments. Then he blew her a last kiss, and waved at the others again, before the train started pulling away from the depot.

Sitting down, he pulled out a book and tried to read it. However, he couldn't concentrate on it, so he put it away again. He relaxed in his seat, shut his eyes, and wished he could shut out the past couple of weeks from his memory.

Ever since he and Lark had first fought about this new post, things had deteriorated between them. Zeb felt like he was making all of the concessions while Lark didn't want to make any. He knew that she was afraid of going to Washington, but he kept trying to reassure her about it. She didn't want to listen, however, saying that children would never survive in Washington, even after he'd outlined all of the advantages Washington held for them.

She kept insisting that they wouldn't be welcomed because of their race. Ever a solution seeker, he'd stopped arguing with her, avoiding her when he could because he knew that she wasn't going to listen to him. Instead of fighting, a useless exercise, he'd decided to do research while he was in Washington, to see what the attitude was like about it. Surely, there had to be other military officers who'd married Indian women.

He would be damned if he was going to let their family be split up. He tried not to think about it, but he had to consider the possibility that Lark wasn't going to move to Washington no matter what. If that was the case, would she move anywhere else? If she hadn't truly been prepared for that possibility, why had she convinced him to marry her?

Maybe she just hadn't thought that far ahead. He hadn't, either, he supposed. All he'd known at the time was that he'd desired her, but then he'd fallen in love with her and their youngsters, and the last thing on his mind had been being transferred somewhere. Truthfully, he'd assumed that Preston would continue to keep him in Echo for years, so he hadn't fully considered what they would do if he was sent to a new post.

As the train rattled eastward, Zeb missed his family more and more with each passing mile. "This is going to be a very, very long trip," he muttered.

"Mother? Mother."

Lark looked up from her desk. Skyhawk stood in front of it.

She smiled at him. "Yes?"

"I need to talk to you," he said in Cheyenne.

Putting aside her work, she gave him her full attention. "Go ahead."

"It is about Washington."

Lark said, "Do not worry, you will not have to go. If Zeb has to take the appointment, we will stay here until you graduate."

He frowned. "Do not make that decision for me. What Zeb will do in Washington is important. If he takes this post, he can help many people, including Indians. If he does, I will go to Washington." He grinned. "Maybe I will be so different and handsome, that those white women will not be able to resist me."

Lark laughed. "You are so humble, my son. They may not even allow you to go to school there or your brother and sisters. I would have to homeschool you."

He cocked his head a little. "Since when have the Cheyenne, or any other Indian tribe, ever backed down from a challenge. I think you are forgetting that I am more man than a boy. With Zeb's help, I can probably get into a school, even if it is not right in the city. Cade says that there are nice places to live that are not in the city."

Lark rubbed her forehead. "Skyhawk, if you have trouble listening to Zeb, how will you deal with teachers? You are not very good at following orders. Have you forgotten how well I know you?"

He gave her a cocky grin. "No, I have not forgotten. I have been doing some thinking and I have learned some things. When I am not constantly irritating Zeb, he is actually a very nice man. I did not give him much of a chance when we first met. I forgot that he is human no matter what color his skin is. He has never done anything to me, except yell at me. But I deserved it."

A sheepish look crossed his face, and she was alarmed when she saw tears in his eyes.

"Why are you crying?"

"Mother, Dog Star and I almost killed Zeb. His fall on the ice was our fault. There was no ice until we poured water on his walkway. We just wanted him to slip a little. It was such a stupid prank and he almost died because of us."

Lark shook her head. "He never told me that. Why would you do such a thing?"

"I will always be sorry for it. Only a few people know that it was our fault. Zeb could have made trouble for me and Dog Star, but he did not. He could have had the military close this school because of what we did, but he did not. He protected us and forgave us. Dog Star paid his restitution, but I have not repaid mine. I could not once I got hurt.

"But I found a way to make restitution to him. If he gets this post, if he wants it, he should take it. I will go to Washington, and you should be willing to as well to show how grateful you are to him that he spared your son and has shown me kindness and love. This is the decision I have made and you will not change my mind. I only have one request, but I will talk to Zeb about it. It will not be for you to decide."

She was taken aback by his story, and by his authoritative attitude. "What is your request?"

"That Dog Star goes with us. He is the brother of my heart, and I am his. I will go whether Zeb grants my request or not, but I will ask just that one last kindness of him. But that is between us men," Skyhawk said, wiping away his tears. "I miss him. I hated him for a long time, and I am ashamed of that now. He is a good man, and you were wise to choose him. I hope he is not long in Washington, so that we can all be together again. I will let you finish your work."

After he left, Lark sat staring at her desk, thinking about everything Skyhawk had just told her. Shame burned through her to know that a fifteen-year-old boy had seen things more clearly than she had. She'd let her own fear cloud her vision concerning the situation. Of course, she hadn't known about the true circumstances around Zeb's accident, either.

Thinking of Skyhawk, she saw that not only had she underestimated

Zeb, she'd underestimated her son, too. If Skyhawk was willing to take a chance on Washington, shouldn't she do the same? Her vision began clearing and she knew what she had to do. She cringed as she relived her and Zeb's horrible fights. So many angry, hurtful words had been exchanged and she'd started to think that their marriage was over when it had barely started.

Skyhawk is right. The Cheyenne do not shy away from adversity. I do not shy away from it. If I had, I would have never found Skyhawk or had the courage to convince Zeb to marry me. I will not give in to fear any longer.

She took some stationary out of her drawer and began writing.

Chapter Twenty-One

Dear Zeb,

Skyhawk told me what you did for the entire school by not letting anyone know that he and Dog Star were responsible for your accident. I'm very grateful for your kindness to the boys, too, and I'm sorry for accusing you of being heartless or a typical military officer. You're neither. You may be a military officer, but you have much more heart than most people know.

I've been such a coward about your new appointment. Skyhawk also told me that he's willing to move to Washington. We underestimated him about some things, one being his ability to be understand the serious nature of the situation and that he would go without causing trouble. I consider myself a coward because I used him as an excuse to not move to Washington.

I'm afraid of not fitting in, of being discriminated against or ostracized. I forgot that I'm the same woman who searched until she found her son. If I can do that, I can live in Washington so that you can do the important work they want you to do. You're right about there being many benefits to living there. I was just too stupid and blind to see them.

I'm seeing clearly now, though, so know that I'll stand by you no matter what happens. That is what a wife is supposed to do, after all. I love you and miss you so much! We all do. I hope all is going well there. Say hello to Preston for us. I'll close, but please know how sorry I am, and that I can't wait to see you again.

All my love,

Lark

P.S. I'll make proper restitution when we're together again.

Zeb sat in Preston's outer lobby waiting to see him. They had a one o'clock appointment, but Preston was running late from another meeting. He smiled as he thought about Lark's letter, and anticipation to rejoin his family gripped him so tightly that he had to shift in his chair a little. There was still a lot for them to discuss, but for the first time since he'd left home, he felt hopeful about the situation.

Finally, Gunther told him to go into Preston's office.

"Thank you, Gunther. I don't envy you your job," he said to the younger man.

Gunther smiled, but wisely refrained from replying one way or another.

Zeb went into Preston's office and sarcastically saluted him.

"Sit your ass in the chair, Captain," Preston said, smiling.

"Yes, sir!" Zeb said and did as ordered.

Preston propped his feet up on his desk. "So what did you want to see me about? I'm a busy man, Zeb."

Zeb got right to it. "I'm throwing myself upon your mercy, and asking that you make this new position go away. I don't want the appointment."

Preston fixed Zeb with a stony glare and lowered his feet to the floor again. "You've got to be kidding me! After all the strings I pulled to get it for you? You moaned about going to Echo and you've been a pain in Arliss and Evan's asses ever since you went there. But, you've done a great job, so after what I considered time served, I decided to get you out of there. Now, you don't want to leave Echo!"

Zeb glowered back at him. "I didn't know you had anything to do with this new assignment! No one told me. I'm not a damn mind reader."

"Of course, I did! I knew you were the right man for the job, so I wheeled-and-dealed to get it for you."

"I appreciate your confidence in me, Preston, but I don't want it."

"Why not, damn it?"

"Because I've forgotten how tedious sitting in meetings is, and I'm not used to being cooped up anymore. I miss riding my horse in the fresh air instead of along a smelly street."

Preston snorted. "The streets don't stink here. We have very good sewage systems."

"You can't sit there and tell me that you don't notice the difference in the air here compared to Echo," Zeb said. "I can and it stinks. I could go on about stuff like that, but the truth is that it's not what's best for my family or for that school, either. All of those kids need Lark and me much more than Washington does and certainly more than I need Washington. You have a choice to make; either I stay in Echo, or I'll resign my commission and retire. I have enough years in to do that."

Preston knew Zeb was serious if he was threatening retirement. He thought of the markers he'd called in and became angry. It was just a good thing that he admired Zeb for what he was doing, or else he'd have demoted Zeb. He also had a fondness for the Echo Indian school, and he'd known that it would be hard to replace Lark with a teacher who would do as well with the children.

He slammed a fist down on his desk. "Gunther! Get in here!"

Zeb raised an eyebrow over Preston's attitude.

Gunther hurried into the room. "Yes, sir?"

Preston wrote furiously on a piece of paper. "Set up a meeting with these people forthwith. Captain Rawlins won't be taking that post after all."

Gunther said, "Yes, sir. I'm sorry to hear that, Captain. It would have been nice having a fri—I'm going right now, sir." He'd caught a dirty look from Preston, and had decided to make a hasty exit.

"Don't think I'm recommending you for another post, Zeb. You cost me too many favors. And, I'm punishing you, too."

Zeb sighed. "I had no doubt that you would. Go ahead."

"Arliss is still in charge of you—"

"Hardly. I don't need him breathing down my neck. I know my job and I don't want his interference," Zeb said.

Preston sent Zeb the toothy smile that always meant that something very unpleasant was about to follow. "You misunderstand me. Arliss is in charge of you, and he and the boys might need your assistance on future assignments. You'll accompany him and do whatever he decides you should do to get the job done."

Zeb said, "You've gone mad! I'm not trained for the sort of thing he does!"

Preston laughed. "If a wealthy rancher and a veterinarian can help him out of some tight spots, I'm sure an army captain can, too."

Zeb ran that over in his mind. "Who do you mean? Who helped him and why?"

"Tell the boys I said it's ok for them to tell you all about it. And stop sticking your nose in Evan's business unless he asks for your help," Preston said. "Now get out and go home. Give my regards to your lovely wife. Why she ever married you, I'll never know."

Zeb smiled. "You might be surprised why. Anyway, I'll remove myself from your presence." Standing, he looked at Preston. "I sincerely thank you, Mr. Secretary."

Preston nodded. "You're welcome. Send Gunther in and tell him to bring that list. I need to make a revision."

"Yes, sir," Zeb said and left.

Gunther came back into the office. "Sir, who are Humphrey Stickyhands and General Killsalot?"

Preston laughed. "Give me that list. It's not real."

Gunther handed it over. "So you don't want me to organize a meeting with these people?"

"You can't organize a meeting with people who don't exist, Gunther. That's what I meant when I said it wasn't real. That'll be all. Thank you," Preston said.

Gunther's bafflement amused Preston, but he held in a laugh until the younger man had left his office.

"And that's why I'm Secretary of War, gentlemen. You can come out now," Preston said.

Arliss came out of Preston's private washroom, a huge smile on his face. "That was pure genius. I'm not sure how I'll use him, but don't worry, I will. He's a good man, Preston. It wasn't nice to dangle that post in front of him like that, though."

"Don't get soft on me now, Arliss. You heard him; he didn't want it anyway."

"It's a good thing he don't know that my codename is Stickyhands and R.J.'s is Killsalot," Arliss said.

Preston laughed. "And he never will. Just like he'll never know that Blake's is Mr. Hardface. Now, on to more pleasant topics. How is Andi?"

Arliss shook his head. "She's not sleeping well. Still having nightmares. She says they're premonitions. That's why I'm asking you for a vacation."

"I thought Evan caught that monster," Preston said.

"Well, they did, but Andi's sure that there's more than one. I need to get home to her. I wouldn't ask, but I need to help figure this out. She's pregnant, and this stress isn't good for either of them."

"Why didn't you say so! Congratulations, Arliss! Oh, wait. Who's the father?" Preston asked, grinning.

Arliss laughed. "He or she might be the only person in history to say that three men helped sire them."

163

"What will they call you all?" Preston asked.

"Well, I'll be Daddy, Blake will be Dad, and R.J. will be Father."

"Your children are going to be very confused unless they're as smart as Andi," Preston said.

"You got that right."

Preston sobered. "Take whatever time you need. I'll consider it still working for me since Skywalker—"

"Skyhawk," Arliss corrected him.

"My apologies. Since Skyhawk was hurt by that maniac, you helping them out will be official business. I can't have my best spy worrying about his wife and child like that. It's too important. Go on home, Arliss, and give Andi my best," Preston said.

Arliss thanked Preston and they shook hands before Arliss left. Preston sighed. There *was* pressing business for Arliss, but he'd meant it when he said that he didn't want Arliss distracted. "Hmm. I wonder if the veterinarian and the rancher would help me out? No one knows about them and they did great work before." Preston tapped his desk for a couple of moments as he considered it. "It wouldn't hurt to ask. Gunther!"

"Is this seat taken?"

Zeb looked up to see Arliss smiling at him. "What are you doing here?" He motioned to the other seat in his compartment.

"I was in town on business," Arliss said, sitting down. "So you turned it down, huh?"

"You must have talked to Preston," Zeb said.

"Yeah. Not long after you did," Arliss said. "I'm headin' home, too. Look, we gotta figure out what's goin' on in Echo."

Zeb frowned. "What do you mean?"

"Ian wasn't the only one responsible for those murders. Andi keeps having premonitions. For her sake and our baby's, we need to wrap this up. She's under too much strain," Arliss said.

"Andi's expecting? I didn't know," Zeb said.

Arliss smiled. "We just found out right before I came here last week. Preston is making this our priority right now and since you work for us, I'm commandeering you to help out. I'll talk to Evan about it. It's not that him and the guys aren't capable, it's that something very strange is going on. Andi's almost always spot on, but whoever's behind all of this is real slick."

Zeb said, "Congratulations, Arliss. I'm very happy for you and Andi. Why haven't you lent your services before now?"

"We haven't been in town much, Zeb. We've been working for Preston. But we need to be home now. It's time for us all to join forces and get this done," Arliss said.

Zeb thought about Skyhawk. "You're right. Enough people have been killed or hurt. We'll get started on it straightaway."

"In the meantime, we're gonna take a nap. Wake us up for supper."

"Sure," Zeb said.

When Arliss' snore filled the compartment, Zeb wanted to kill him. Instead, he turned Arliss out by concentrating on his family, and imagining what they'd been doing since he'd been gone. After a while, he slept, dreaming of his loved ones in Echo.

Epilogue

Lark started when someone shook her. Rolling over she saw a man standing by the bed and let out a cry of fright, before throwing a punch at him.

"Ouch! It's just me," Zeb said.

"Zeb? What are you doing here? You didn't send word that you were coming home! You can't do that!" Lark wrapped her arms around herself.

Zeb lit a lamp and saw the terror in her eyes. "I'm so sorry," he said, sitting down by her.

Lark practically launched herself at him, breaking into sobs. "I'm so glad you're home. I missed you so much and I'm so sorry for everything I said to you."

"Shh, honey. I got your letter. It's all right now. I wasn't very nice, either. I'm just so happy to see you again," he said.

She held him tightly, pressing a kiss to his cheek before drawing back and kissing him. "I love you and I'm ready to move to Washington."

He smiled. "We're not moving to Washington."

"Yes, we are. I told you that we were so you can take this post and we can all be together. You're not giving it up. It's too important," Lark said. "So do we need to start packing right away?"

166

"No, Lark. We're not moving. I turned it down. I don't want it," he said.

"It's because of me, isn't it? Just tell them that you changed your mind," Lark said. "I don't want you to resent us by not taking it. Besides, they need you."

Zeb took her hands and shook them a little. "Lark, please listen to me. I appreciate your willingness to go. I really do, but the truth is that I really don't want to go to Washington. If this had come along a couple of years ago, I would have jumped at the chance, but not now."

"I don't understand. Why not?"

"Because when those two hooligans almost killed me, a miracle happened. If they hadn't pulled that prank on me, I wouldn't have had the opportunity to get to know everyone as a person. I wouldn't have had the chance to get to know myself as a person instead of just a soldier. That's all I was for so long, that I didn't know what it was like to be just Zeb Rawlins.

"I certainly wouldn't have become a father or have married the most beautiful, kind, contrary woman I've ever met. So, almost dying was a blessing in disguise. I missed you all so much and I missed Echo, too. I'm happy here and I don't want to go anywhere else. Besides, no one else could be the kind of teacher these kids need, ours included," Zeb said.

Lark brushed a lock of dark hair off his forehead and caressed his cheek. "Are you absolutely sure?" she asked.

"I'm positive. All I want is to keep doing what we're doing now. I'm the happiest I've ever been and I don't want anything to ruin that," he replied.

"All right. It was a miracle for me, too, you know. If you hadn't gotten knocked on the head, I would have kept on hating you. I'm glad that I got to know the man under the uniform in more ways than one," she said with a wicked little smile.

He chuckled. "Me, too. Believe me."

"Am I forgiven?"

"Mmm, almost," he said. "I believe there's the matter of restitution to be paid."

Lark laughed. "I'll make good on that, but will you just hold me for a while?"

He saw the frightened look return to her eyes. "What's happened?"

"There's another reason I was so scared when you woke me up." Her eyes filled with tears. "There's been another murder."

Zeb felt the blood drain from his face. "Oh, no. Who?"

A sob escaped her. "Ellie."

Zeb's shock was so complete that he couldn't speak for several moments. "*Our* Ellie?"

Lark nodded. "Yes. She went out the other night with Jerry and Sonya to Spike's. She went to use the washroom, but she didn't come back. They started hunting for her right away, but they didn't find her until yesterday. Dog Star found her body in the barn yesterday morning when he went to feed the horses."

The hair on the back of Zeb's neck rose at the thought that the killer had been on their property. "Good God," he said. "Is everyone else all right?"

She nodded. "Yes, but Dog Star is terrified to go to the barn by himself now. This is two bodies he's come across, and after what happened with Skyhawk—well, you can understand."

"Yes, I can. I'll be back. I want to talk to Cade a moment. He should just be heading out on patrol," he said.

"Ok."

After conferring with Cade for twenty minutes about taking more precautions and adjusting their patrol schedule, Zeb went upstairs and checked on all of the kids, quietly entering their rooms and making sure their windows were locked. When he got to Skyhawk and Dog Star's room, he knocked softly before going on in, not wanting to scare them.

Skyhawk rose up on an elbow. "Zeb? Are you really here or am I dreaming?"

Zeb smiled. "I'm really here. I missed you."

"You did? I missed you, too. I wish you'd have come home sooner," Skyhawk said.

Zeb heard someone sniff on his right. "Dog Star?"

"Yeah."

Zeb sat down on the boy's bed and ran a hand over his silky hair. "It's ok, Dog Star. We're going to catch whoever did this. Don't be afraid."

Dog Star shook his head. "I can't help it. I can't sleep because I see Ellie hanging there and I'm scared that they're gonna get in here and—"

Zeb embraced him. "I know you've been through some traumatic experiences the past several months, but I promise you that we'll catch them. Until we do, we'll make absolutely certain that you're all safe."

Dog Star hung onto him and let out his fear and grief, something he hadn't fully done yet. "I'm sorry. I should be stronger," he said pulling back in a few minutes.

"Dog Star, there's nothing wrong with being frightened," Zeb said.

Dog Star took the handkerchief Zeb gave him and blew his nose. "You're never afraid."

Zeb laughed. "I'm scared a lot."

Skyhawk said, "You are? Why? You're a tough army captain."

"Thanks, but even tough captains are allowed to be scared. Although, I will say that I have a lot more to be scared about since you two pulled that stunt on me," he said, chuckling.

Dog Star asked, "What are you afraid of?"

"Well, as I just told Lark, a miracle happened, and now I have all of you crazy kids and a beautiful woman to love. I don't want anything to happen to all of my miracles, so I'm going to turn that fear into determination," Zeb said. "And, I'm sure that the sheriff and his men are doing the same. Determination comes from fear, anger or a combination thereof, gentleman. So, what we're going to do is use them to work hard to make things safe around here again. And you two will help with that, starting tomorrow."

"We are?" Dog Star said. "How can we help?"

"I'll show you in the morning, but for now, get some sleep. Rest easy, Dog Star. You're safe," Zeb said.

Dog Star lay back down. "Ok. Thanks."

"You, too, Skyhawk," Zeb said.

"Ok. Goodnight."

"Goodnight."

Towards morning as Zeb and Lark held each other, he watched the sun come up and looked down at Lark, one of the many miracles that had been granted him. He smiled as he thought about the restitution she'd paid him, but his happiness went much deeper than anything physical.

This was where he was meant to be, there in Echo, guarding an Indian school. After his previous military assignments, it had seemed a lowly post, but now, he thought it was the best post he would ever have, and he planned to keep it as long as possible. To that end, he would do whatever it took to catch the killer among them.

Letting go of that for the moment, he kissed the top of Lark's head, and tightened his arms around her.

"Are you all right?" he asked. He knew she wasn't asleep.

"Yes. Just listening to your heartbeat. I like hearing it."

If she was one of Zeb's miracles, he was certainly one of hers. She found it nothing short of miraculous to have found a man so generous, strong, and loving. The Great Spirit had brought them together, and had given them even more miracles in the forms of children. She couldn't imagine her life without any of them now, nor did she want to.

"I hate you," she said.

Zeb chuckled. "I hate you, too."

She giggled and said, "I hope you know how much I hate you."

"Oh, yes. You've shown me several times how much you hate me. I hope you know how much I hate you, too."

"I'm not sure if I do."

"Hmm. Well, then let me show you again, so you fully understand."

She giggled as he kissed her. They were startled by a knock on their bedroom door and broke apart.

"Hang on," Zeb called, pulling on a pair of pants quickly, while Lark put on her nightgown and robe.

"*Ného'e!*" Gray Dove shouted when he opened the door.

She was followed by Dewdrop and Jumper. They mobbed Zeb and he embraced all of his little miracles, kissing them and teasing them. He and Lark exchanged a loving look and then went to help make breakfast, rejoicing that their family was back together once again.

Shadow barely got one step inside the door of the sheriff's office before Evan bellowed, "Don't touch anything!"

Shadow gazed around at the office in wonderment. All of the furniture and the floor was covered with evidence from the serial murder case.

"Have you been here all night?" he asked.

"Yeah. It's here. I know it is. I just have to see it all the right way," Evan said, distractedly. His urgency was almost palpable.

Shadow went to hang up his coat, but then noticed that a blanket hung on the coatrack. Carefully, he tiptoed around the paraphernalia on the floor until he reached his desk. He draped his coat over his chair and carefully sat down on it since there wasn't anything on the seat.

Evan picked up the bottle of whiskey on his desk and took a healthy swig. "I just have to see it right. It's not in the right order."

Taking in Evan's disheveled appearance and slightly glazed eyes, Shadow grew concerned for his boss. "Are you all right?"

"Hell, no, I'm not all right!" Evan yelled. "I've got another friggin' madman on the loose, another woman is dead, and a whole town full of people are scared out of their minds! Of course I'm not all right!"

Thad walked in the door. He took one look at the scene before him, and knew what was happening. Evan was doing what he called, "drink until I see it," something he only did when he was desperate to solve a crime. It had been a long time since Thad had seen Evan play it, though. Calmly, he walked over to his desk, and asked, "Can I move this drawing?"

Evan glanced at it. "Yeah. Just sit it on top of the other one there."

Thad sat down and lit a cigarette. "Ok, Sheriff. Tell me what you're thinkin'."

"It's here, Thad. It's right in front of my face, but I can't see it!"

Thad said, "Then rearrange it, son."

Shadow watched Evan scurry around the office, moving papers and evidence around. Judging from Thad's reaction to Evan's odd behavior, this was something the two men had done before. When he was finished, Evan drank more whiskey and closed his eyes. After a few moments, he reopened them and began going over the evidence again. He arrived at the long table in the center of the room and something caught his eye. He pulled over his desk chair and stood on it, looking down at the papers laid out on the table.

"Who drew this?" he demanded, snatching up a piece of paper, and showing it to them.

Shadow said, "I did."

"When?"

"Right after we found the original six women," Shadow replied.

"I could kiss you right now, but that's only because I'm drunk. I knew I'd see it! I knew it had to be here," Evan said.

He ran to his desk, grabbing a tablet and a pencil. Placing Shadow's drawing next to the tablet, he copied it over onto a clean sheet of paper and held it up to them. He'd used a large, shaded-in circle to denote a woman's body.

"Looks random, doesn't it?"

Both deputies agreed.

"It's not. Watch."

Evan connected the circles with heavy lines and held the drawing up again. "And now?"

"A chalice," Shadow said. "Are we looking for a Christian now instead of a Satanic worshipper?"

Evan laughed. "Nope. There are Wiccan religions that use a chalice. They're different than Satanists. People get them confused. Wiccans are mainly peaceful, but like in any religion, there are people who twist it to suit whatever their sick objective might be. I think that's what's happened here.

"In some Wiccan sects, the chalice represents fertility, the womb, and gestation. All of the victims have been brunettes, except Ellie. She was blonde. I need to know Erin's autopsy results, but I'm betting that she doesn't have a symbol on her. She wasn't buried like the others."

Thad shook his head. "You lost me, Evan, and I can usually follow you."

"Think about it, Thad! We killed one of the killers. Ellie doesn't follow the pattern of the other women! Look across the top of the drawing. It needs one more victim to finish the top of the chalice. There should be one more woman there.

"Why didn't he take Ellie to finish it?" Evan continued. "Because she was used as revenge for us killing this maniac's partner. Maybe the two lunatics are even related. They hung Ellie where they knew she would be found. They wanted to show everyone that they're still here and that they're pissed off. They're gonna try to murder another woman, and I know who it's gonna be."

"Who?" Shadow asked.

"He's looking for a pregnant brunette to finish the symbol. It must be a part of some sort of spell," Evan said, sitting down heavily in his chair, exhausted from being up all night and all of the mental energy he'd expended on the situation.

Thad and Shadow looked at each other with stunned expressions.

Thad said, "Molly's a pregnant brunette."

"So is Bree and both of them are showing now," Shadow said.

Evan nodded. "I know. You better make sure they don't go anywhere alone, gentlemen."

Thad said, "Wait a minute, Evan. What about Skyhawk? He's definitely not gonna be havin' a baby. Why did they want him?"

"He stumbled into an area that he wasn't supposed to. The traps were laid to prevent anyone from finding something, not just him. That's why Ian tracked him down to Mr. March's cabin. They don't want any witnesses and they wanted to make sure that Skyhawk was silenced.

"We have to go back to where he got caught in that trap and have a look around in the daylight. Ellie could also have been meant as a warning to those boys to stay away and keep their mouths shut," Evan said, looking around at the mess he'd made.

"Help me clean this up, fellas. Then go make sure your women are all right. I'll go get Lucky and meet you out where Skyhawk was hurt. We're also gonna have another chat with Mr. March."

The three of them quickly completed the task. As the men left the office and went their separate ways, Evan's determination to solve the mystery grew into an obsession. He mounted his horse and rode away with a cruel smile on his face.

"You didn't think I'd be smart enough to figure it out, did you, jackass?" he muttered a little drunkenly to himself. "Guess what? I did and no matter what I have to do, I'm gonna take you down. You wanna play hide-and-go-seek? Fine by me. Ready or not, here I come!"

The End

Thank you for reading and supporting my book and I hope you enjoyed it. Please will you do me a favor and leave me a review, so I'll know whether you liked it or not, it would be very much appreciated, thank you.

Linda's Other Books

Dawson Chronicles Series

Mistletoe Mayhem
  (Dawson Chronicles Book 1)
After The Storm
  (Dawson Chronicles Book 2)

Echo Canyon Brides Series

Montana Rescue
  (Echo Canyon brides Book 1)
Montana Bargain
  (Echo Canyon brides Book 2)
Montana Adventure
  (Echo Canyon brides Book 3)
Montana Luck
  (Echo Canyon brides Book 4)
Montana Fire
  (Echo Canyon brides Book 5)
Montana Hearts
  (Echo Canyon brides Book 6)

Montana Hearts
  (Echo Canyon brides Book 7)
Montana Orphan
  (Echo Canyon brides Book 8)
Montana Surprise
  (Echo Canyon Brides Book 9)
Montana Miracle
  (Echo Canyon Brides Book 10)

Montana Mail Order Brides Series

Westward Winds
  (Montana Mail Order brides Book 1)
Westward Dance
  (Montana Mail Order brides Book 2)
Westward Bound
  (Montana Mail Order brides Book 3)

Westward Destiny
  (Montana Mail Order brides
  Book 4)
Westward Fortune
  (Montana Mail Order brides
  Book 5)
Westward Justice
  (Montana Mail Order brides
  Book 6)
Westward Dreams
  (Montana Mail Order brides
  Book 7)
Westward Holiday
  (Montana Mail Order brides
  Book 8)
Westward Sunrise
  (Montana Mail Order brides
  Book 9)
Westward Moon
  (Montana Mail Order brides
  Book 10)
Westward Christmas
  (Montana Mail Order brides
  Book 11)
Westward Visions
  (Montana Mail Order brides
  Book 12)
Westward Secrets
  (Montana Mail Order brides
  Book 13)

Westward Changes
  (Montana Mail Order brides
  Book 14)
Westward Heartbeat
  (Montana Mail Order brides
  Book 15)
Westward Joy
  (Montana Mail Order brides
  Book 16)
Westward Courage
  (Montana Mail Order brides
  Book 17)
Westward Spirit
  (Montana Mail Order brides
  Book 18)
Westward Fate
  (Montana Mail Order brides
  Book 19)
Westward Hope
  (Montana Mail Order brides
  Book 20)
Westward Wild
  (Montana Mail Order brides
  Book 21)
Westward Sight
  (Montana Mail Order brides
  Book 22)
Westward Horizons
  (Montana Mail Order brides
  Book 23)

Cast of Characters

Tim Dwyer-son of Joe and Lacey Dwyer

Renee Keller- Switch and Hope Keller's daughter

Switch and Hope Keller

Skip Keller-Renee's younger brother

Jethro Keller-Renee's older brother

Sawyer Samuels-owns the Shutter Shoppe

Devon Samuels-Sawyer's wife

Dr. Marcus Samuels-Head doctor at Dawson Community Hospital

Dr. Mike Samuels-Marcus' nephew

Chief Black Fox

Raven Dwyer and Zoe Dwyer-Hailey and Dusty's parents

Dusty Dwyer- Raven's son

Hailey Dwyer- Raven's daughter

Joe and Lacey Dwyer

Joey and Snow Song Dwyer

Kyle Dwyer-Son of Joe and Lacey Dwyer

Art Perrone- Kyle's buddy from the war

Minx-Reckless' sister

Emily Night Sky-Joe and Lacey's daughter

Jasmine Night Sky-Bobby and Emily's daughter

Hunter Night Sky- Jasmine's younger brother

Brown Otter- Black Fox's son-in-law

Matt "Mac" Mackenzie

Randy Cooper-son of Chester and Letty Cooper

Randall and Edwina Cranston

Cora Ambrose-Joe and Lacey's cook and friend

Jake Henderson

Andy Henderson-Jake's son

Mitch Taylor

Shawn Taylor

Dash- Skip's draft mule

Connect With Linda

Visit my website at **www.lindabridey.com** to view my other books and to sign up to my mailing list so that you are notified about my new releases.

About Linda Bridey

LINDA BRIDEY lives in New Mexico with her three dogs; a German shepherd, chocolate Labrador retriever, and a black Pug. She became fascinated with Montana and decided to combine that fascination with her fictional romance writing. Linda chose to write about mail-order-brides because of the bravery of these women who left everything and everyone to take a trek into the unknown. The Westward series books are her first publications.

Made in the USA
Monee, IL
22 August 2020